PLATEAU SURFERS:
THE EXPLANATION OF IT ALL

CODY TESNOW

PublishAmerica
Baltimore

First printing

ISBN: 1-4137-5478-3
PUBLISHED BY PUBLISHAMERICA, LLLP
www.publishamerica.com
Baltimore

Printed in the United States of America

This book is dedicated to several people, as it should be, as it is my first book. First, to my editor, who helped me "check my ego" in order to make this a better book. Second, to all my friends and family, whom all know their part and influence with both me and this book. Third, to you, the reader, for reading books instead of watching TV. Also, to anyone who wants peace and goodwill towards all, and recognizes the absurdity and humor that is everywhere in life.

Thank you all.

REALLY! You should stop and read…

…the Preface/Disclaimer

More things on this planet, but especially words, should come with disclaimers. The following is this particular book's disclaimer. The following words are a work of fact and fiction. It is not remotely the authors duty or responsibility to separate the two. These words are neither true nor false, but written entirely for entertainment, yours and mine. It is not the author's responsibility if the following words make you happy or sad, sedated or furious. It is not the authors concern if you find the words offensive, or if you are offended by their un-offensiveness. They are not intended to be wise or foolish, sacrilegious or divine, cruel or passionate. They are not intended to make you a better person, or a worse person, or the same you were before you read them in the first place. The only thing that these words really have the power to do is make you think about them, and after that, the author is free of any accountability. See? Painless. You may continue.

CHAPTER 1
ON DEATH AND ALIENS

Most people don't realize that it is very difficult to die. It takes most people an average of 84.7 years to get it done. That is, of course, barring any accidents, child deaths, murders, suicides, and miscellaneous deaths of unnatural circumstances, but including terminal and non-terminal diseases, cancer, AIDS, and the like. One person, who was exceptionally bad at dying, lived to be 120! Many people, also terrible at death, live past 100 years old, ten decades, a century! The only things on earth worse than Humans at death are certain tortoises and trees. Maybe the Loch Ness Monster and a few other such creatures…but pound for pound, Humans are by far the worst at death on this little blue orb.

Humans also are by far more responsible for Human death than all the other causes combined.

For the most part, since Humans are so bad at death, many of them don't think about it until it happens. Still, many others, arrogant and proud, think that they are so good, so fantastic at death, that they worry about it all the time.

Still others, so concerned with Human death, feel they have to help the others along, so they build nasty bombs and bugs, start wars and hand out silly substances that help everybody out.

Out. The key word.

How many people have been on Earth? Some say as many as 5 trillion. 5,000,000,000,000! 5,000 billions! Holy moly! Now, my non-expert guess would be that 2.5 trillion of those people's skills in death were improved by the other half. And the other Creatures say...

...Oh well.

There are, in this author's humble, yet informed, opinion undoubtedly Aliens. In the true-blue, dyed-in-the-wool, saucer-flying little-green-men-who-communicate-telepathically sense. There are also undoubtedly other creatures who look exactly like us from other planets, solar systems, galaxies. Also, globs of sentient slime, beings that exist only as energy, hairy ape creatures with advanced science, and barely conscious creatures that don't really know about anything but themselves.

Incidentally, you can find all these Creatures right here on Earth as well. You don't need to go muck around Space.

Watch a science fiction movie. When you see an animal from another planet you are sure to say, "Woo! Look at that thing that looks like a cat-dog-octopus! Nothing could ever look so strange!"

Have you ever really looked at an octopus? Or a platypus? Odds on that you have eaten chicken. Have you ever seen a real live chicken? Aliens from all over would be sure to say, "What? You EAT that?"

Once I read this great line in a very famous comic strip, since discontinued: "The only proof that there is intelligent extraterrestrial life is that they haven't visited us."

Imagine yourself an Alien flying across the Galaxy in your super-space-travel device, whatever that may be, and it comes across this planet with all these animals on it, the large majority of which are buzzing, annoying, disease-carrying creatures flying all around. And then you have your insects, of course. Then other mammals, fish, birds, plants, and the like, all of which are equally strange, not to mention that the place itself seems to be getting sick, scarred and torn, scabbed and festering, seemingly healthy in some spots, but obviously dying in others...are you going to stop?

Insects outweigh Humans ten pounds to one. Or something like that.

Humans are the only Creatures that don't use 100 percent of their brain. Take dolphins for instance. A dolphin's brain is very much like a Humans. Similar in size, weight, and similar fold depth, which I am told is the important thing. What do dolphins do all day? They swim in the ocean, which they do not now nor ever have polluted; they play; they eat; they sleep; they make babies (but not too many); and they never, ever fight amongst themselves. I just have this feeling that dolphins are always making fun of Humans. They probably have jokes about Humans like Humans tell about other Humans. (I don't think dolphins make fun of each other.) Only I think their jokes may make them shake their head more than laugh.

Q: How many Humans does it take to catch a fish for dinner?
A: Too many.

Dolphin humor is seldom funny to Humans, I suppose.

A note to readers: 85% of all statistics are made up on the spot. I am always making things up. Really, you shouldn't believe a word I say. A good dictionary, an encyclopedia, and perhaps a fast Internet connection would be helpful in distinguishing fact from fiction for the above "facts" and anything else I might say that comes under scrutiny throughout my story. You heard it here first.

I have been told by several Creatures of Earth that Math is the Universal Language of the Universe. HA!

The Universal Language of the Universe was most definitely not discovered, created, or otherwise figured out by Humans.

They are not that smart.

And, the Universal Language of the Universe is most certainly not the numbered system that just happens to be agreed on by most of the communicating members of Earth. Notice I said "most." I am quite sure there have been wars fought over Math.

The only way I might be wrong on this subject is if the Universal Language of the Universe is Music.

Of course, Humans are extremely close-minded about Music. Most of the time, they can't hear it anyway, and even more so, when they do hear it, they can't all agree on whether or not it is Music. I once had an argument with a person who was quite sure that animals never made Music. They said that was only their way of communicating. My point exactly!

So, Aliens, not at all unlike dolphins, probably think we are silly, and perhaps only occasionally play with us, out of sheer boredom.

Dolphins most certainly have no interest in having Humans come swim with them, and anyone who thinks otherwise is right out of their tree.

Humans, who are at best, clunky, bad-swimmers with too much hair and no sense of humor or direction, not to mention flopping shark treats, of course all think otherwise.

CHAPTER 2
ALL ABOUT ME,
AND THE TITLE EXPLAINED

By this point in the story, you may be wondering who yours truly is, or what yours truly is, for that matter. Is he (she, it?) an animal, vegetable or mineral? Of Earth or not? The answer, of course, is yes. All and none of the above. Definition of any Being is almost always impossible within the scope of one word, and this, of course, is part of Humanity's problem. We are all complex individuals, no two really alike.

And we know it.

Knowledge of individuality has been the downfall of more societies than any other, I suppose. As soon as a Creature figures out that it really is a singular being, it also supposes that it must protect itself at all costs, including but not limited to removing all possible threats by subversion or force or some other fashion in which said individual helps others along in some way or another, teaching them how to be better at death. And usually, and even more problematic, a group of people finds out that they are separate and not equal from all other groups, and this is where the problems really begin.

But back to me.

I think that a being is defined by what it believes in congruence with how it acts. I happen to do lots of things, and write these things down. I also think a lot. So I will tell you what I think, which is, for lack of a better word, phrase, language, whatever, what I believe. Certainly I think about things that I do not believe, but this immediately brings to surface what I do believe, and BAM! My point is made.

I find myself being dismissed quite often.

To be a little less evasive, I will tell you that I am an observer. I look at things, not from a better place, but from a different place. This is a place where some Creatures get confused. I have an opinion on every subject, regardless of my knowledge of it. I also have a personal solution for every problem. If everyone would listen to me and only me, things would be peachy.

Sounds a bit Human, doesn't it?

Don't let that sidetrack you.

There are others like me, each of us, of course, beautiful, individual flowers, all intelligent, and generally friendly creatures. We are often seen as rude, which is what you are when you tell someone how you really feel. We are also seen as arrogant, which is what you are when you think for yourself. We are also seen as and thus called several other nasty names, none of which are really things applicable in the first place, other than the fact that the purporter of these charges and names think that they are insults.

Of course, we think we are always right about things that matter, and are much more likely to tell you so than blow our own horn when we are wrong, which, like all other creatures, we so often are, but we'll be damned if we're going to let you throw a party about it.

And we have a name, that we gave ourselves (all the outside suggestions, were, well...somewhat derogatory.) And if you hadn't already guessed...that name is...

Plateau Surfers. Our motto is:

"Not a better view, just a different one."

And Thus the Title Is Explained.

CHAPTER 3
ONE MORE THING BEFORE YOU GO ON...

For those of you wondering, this will indeed turn into a story with Characters, including myself and a few others with whom my paths will cross, or not, depending on how you view the fiction/nonfiction issue. But before that Story can begin, there must be two more points made, and points of the type I find Humans get so perturbed about so quickly.

Point 1: This is similar to a point in the Preface/Disclaimer, but bear with me. This Story will undoubtedly conflict with a belief or two of yours. Please don't let this affect your mood while reading, remember, it's just a Story.

Sub Point 1: During Point 2, please refer to Point 1, if necessary.

Point 2: The Author/Speaker/Main Character of this Story does not believe in the Human god, God, or any faith-based manifestation thereof. This may or may not be cleared up later. However, it needed to be pointed out so that the Story can begin as it needs to begin. It should also be pointed out that a belief in a god will not affect whether or not the Story can or can not be entertaining. The Story is just fine with higher powers, and Humans being created, but not OK with God as Supreme Ruler of the Universe, and God as a Man or Woman, or as any personification or animification of something that, were it to exist in the first place, would be completely intangible, unnamable, and so on and so forth.

Well, enough on that.

CHAPTER 4
AND SO THE STORY BEGINS...

Once upon a time, there was a Universe. This Universe was one of countless others, and within this particular Universe, there were countless Galaxies, each with countless Stars and countless Solar Systems and countless Planets, and countless Civilizations each with countless Creatures in it, around it, and so on and so forth.

So, pretty much, no number could suffice to match the number of Creatures in It All. Not even if I wrote the number "1" and followed it by 100 pages of zeros.

But it is also important to point out that it was not an Infinite number. There is very little that is Infinite. I would go so far as to say nothing is Infinite, but that seems premature. For instance, one particular item which many think is Infinite is most definitely not. Time. Time, while certainly seemingly Infinite, is actually a very, very large circle.

Very large.

There is no way of measuring The Circle, and there is no distance you could get from the circle where any given point did not look like a very straight line, unless, of course, you could get out to one perpendicular endpoint of the radius of this Time Circle, but let's be serious here.

It's just really big.

Now, what happens when the Time Circle completes? Nobody knows, because honestly, nobody I nor anyone I know knows anyone who has lived long enough to even feel it start to bend.

So, suffice to say, our story begins on a little blue orb in a Solar System in a Galaxy in a Universe in It All. Far away. And fairly unimportant in the Grand Scheme of Things, but again, what isn't?

So, we're on Earth, right?

Sorry, not yet.

On this particular little blue orb, there were all sorts of creatures, which were not at all unlike you and the things you know.

It had been around for millions of years, and its inhabitants really had no clue as to how it or they got there, but they sure did have their ideas about it. This place had animals and plants and businesses and things not at all unlike buses, and grocery stores and parks and so on and so forth.

Humanoid, we'll say.

Now, this group has had its problems. Slavery, for one, in its past, and now all but forgotten, because they really aren't any smarter than Humans.

Now, as it happens, or as I was told, these Creatures were bound to their world by a similar Law to your Gravity. (Another seemingly

Infinite rule, that as you will find out sooner than later, is about as Infinite as a Popsicle.) So, thousands and thousands of years go by with these Creatures walking around, shooting themselves off into the sky and Space, and generally thinking they were the Masters of All They Surveyed, and that they were unique little flowers, and that they were more than likely alone in It All.

Alone, of course, except that they were created by some Great Being that loved them and only them, and even then, some of them were quite certain that It loved a certain section of them, and only loved that section. Other sections disagreed, and they fought and bickered and caused problems.

Sounds familiar? Don't get ahead of yourself.

So, one day on this little blue orb, a child was born. Now, this was hardly a big event, as this particular group of Creatures was quite adept at filling up its little blue orb. But this child was different, because it decided that it was not going to obey all the rules.

This child could fly.

Of course, this was a huge phenomenon at first, but after a few thousand years, almost everyone on the planet could fly, and those who could not were ridiculed and put into slavery, because face it, they still hadn't learned anything.

Then one day another child was born.

This particular child decided that it was going to defy even more rules, and that it was just going to stop paying attention to any rules of Physics and so on and so forth whatsoever, and would just de-atomize himself, move those atoms to where ever it saw fit, put them back together, and, well, POOF!

Flying was a thing of the past. Few thousand years go by, birth becomes easier, but it was also very easy to be good at death, and wars were messy, and of course, if you could only fly? Forget about it…you were ridiculed and put into slavery, because let's face it, they still hadn't learned anything.

Then what?

Well, of course another child was born…but not really. It just came out existing as pure energy. And it went on its merry way. Few thousand years later, everyone is practically gone, save a few De-Atomizers who pretty much have the run of the place. And they have learned their lesson, having been slaves and all. Their little blue orb has nearly repaired itself, and all the Creatures on it live in harmony, and aren't lazy about things like recycling and alternate energy sources…oh no…they won't forget how to be nice to each other and their home for at least a few thousand years.

And what about everybody else?
Really, we are only concerned with one of these Creatures. One day, while flitting around it's Galaxy, or perhaps another one, who knows, it comes across this little blue orb. Something is fairly familiar about this place, and so, without much ado, it plants it with what cannot be called anything but the Seeds of Life, and goes on its merry way.

Give yourself a few thousand, or million, or billion years, whatever you subscribe to, and BAM! There you are.

Now we're on Earth.

CHAPTER 5
AND NOW THE CHARACTERS

Every Story must have its Characters, and this Story is no different. I would let you meet the Characters one by one, as they enter into the story, and of course they will, here and there, but nobody needs or wants a Main Character jumping out of thin air and surprising them. So, on with it then.

First, there is me. I am not a "Main Character," so much as Narrator. I have my part in the Story, and have several literary moments all to myself, but I am less integral to the action of the story than others. I have seen and experienced the Story as it took place and have compiled more stories through conversation with characters after the fact. To say that I am connected to the story is both true and absurd, as you will find we are all quite connected, both through the story and otherwise. As observer and interacter, however, I must have a name, by which you can identify me. So we don't have other Characters saying things like "Hey Observer/Author/Thingy, did you hear the one about..." and other such nonsense. From henceforth, then, you will know me as Os.

✦
✦ ✦

And now…

The Cast (More or Less…)

Anthony - Has a Band. An Alien Band. No one mistakes him for normal.

Dan - An anal-retentive medical student who discovers something important to the Story.

Greg - An altruistic egotist, if there is such a thing…a cynic with a soul.

Isabella - A child who quite accidentally saves the Earth, at the very least.

Jack - Isabella's mother, a woman who will begin to wish there weren't Aliens.

Joe - An innocuous name for an innocuous fellow. Joe is most definitely an Alien. In the sense that he is not of Earth, anyway.

Josh - An Alien Warrior with a soft spot for kittens. Really.

Justin - An Otherworldly Bartender who can give strangely relevant advice at crucial moments.

Neil - Part Human, part, well…who knows…but a very important fellow. He loves to sing.

Terry - A Human Writer with a love of the pen and the bottle…always writes the Truth, but no one believes him.

Tony - The cosmic equivalent of the love child of Danny Devito and Woody Allen. 100% Neurotic heart. Alien doesn't even begin to describe it.

Certainly, there are others, but these are the real meat and potatoes here. The ones you should commit to memory.

On with the Story.

CHAPTER 6
OATMEAL

Now, as you may well know, from reading other stories (if this is your first, I am sorry on so many levels), usually the Storyteller introduces the Characters through the story rather than before. This is a fine way to do things. Myself, I will do it both ways, if you don't mind.

Everyone talks about knowing where they were when That Big Something happens. They were buying coffee, they were sleeping, they were dancing the fandango with a mongoose, whatever. Being the observer I am, I just happen to know this for myself and for everyone else involved.

Makes it easy to tell the story, you see.

Not only that, but I know what they were doing before and after as well. Although, after is hardly important to this story, seeing that The Big Something is rather, well…

…let's not get ahead of ourselves.

The thing about this "Big Something" is that it is not a specific time and place, like so many other "Big Somethings." This is important to remember.

Really, I am just telling you all this so we can be clear on how things work around here. Once we have all the Rules of the Story straightened out, it makes things go so much more smoothly.

It should also be noted that I, as the Storyteller, am allowed to break any rules I see necessary. One of the perks.

So, for the next few chapters of The Story, you will have to read (and pay close attention to) everyone's story, how they affect each other, and realize the Cosmic Importance of each of the Characters. And also one other thing.

It would all be over for all of us, and I don't just mean "us" as the Characters, I mean all of us, as far as I can tell, if it weren't for oatmeal.

CHAPTER 7
WHERE I WAS, WHAT I WAS DOING

In a cave, eating oatmeal. Completely unaware, at the time, of the considerable impact of this particular grain cereal. I was eating my oatmeal with a chutney of apples and raisins, boiled in a spiced apple cider, and reduced to a sauce. It's quite delicious. Anyway, back to the cave. Why I was in a cave is not terribly important, but important enough to tell you that the cave was in the desert, and I was in it.

Sometimes, you just have to be by yourself, you know? Get away from it all.

What I was, and you are, soon to find out was that my breakfast would soon do me considerably more good than getting my daily fiber.

Now, I am not sure how much you, as a person, know about the Pyramids. Sure, you know what they look like, and you might know some of the names of some of them, and you might know there are more than one, that they are very big, and they may or may not bring to mind the Egyptians.

What I know, and you are soon to know, is that the Egyptians have about as much to do with building the Pyramids as you do with the building of the Rocky Mountains. And if you did build the Rocky Mountains, you should be doing something better with your time than reading this Story.

Some Facts on the Pyramids

(significantly, specifically, the Great Pyramid at Giza)

The Pyramid is located at the exact center of Earth's land mass.

It can be seen from space.

The height of the Pyramid's apex is 5,812.98 inches, and each side is 9,131 inches from corner to corner. Divide the circumference of the Pyramid by twice its height, the result is 3.14159, or pi.

Add all the sides of the Pyramid, and you get 36,524. Move your decimal, dividing by 100. Number of days in a year. (On Earth, anyway.)

The average height of land mass above sea level, measurable now by lots of smart people with lots of free time, is roughly 5,450 inches at this time in our lives. Four thousand years ago, it is speculated, that due to less water in the oceans, (our ice caps have melted a bit), that number was closer to 5,800 inches. Pretty close to the height of the Great Pyramid, no?

So, there are some, including me, and soon to be you, who know that the Pyramids were built as "land markers."

Your first thought might be the same as mine. Why would Aliens build a pyramid using the English inch?

Quite frankly…they didn't. Humans, of course, have been using the "Alien Inch" for the last thousand years, and before that, it didn't exist, as far as Humans were concerned.

The truth of the matter is that there are several species of Aliens who think since their way is the right way, and all other ways are silly and need to be eradicated, that they go ahead and introduce their idea to us Humans, in such a manner we have no choice but to use it.

Sounds familiar, doesn't it?

So, there I am, in a cave, in the desert.

My cave just happens to be directly adjacent to a Pyramid in the middle of the Sahara. I only found it by accident, and happen to be the first on Earth to ever set foot inside this particular Pyramid. What I will find out later, and tell you now, is this is the first Pyramid ever built.

And therefore, and obviously, Important.

I had found the Pyramid, after some considerable happenstance, not in Egypt, but in the African country of Mali, right in the middle of the Sahara desert, and not on the equator, but on the Prime Meridian, west of Kidal, east of Mabrouk. These things are hardly important.

The important thing is that I was in the cave, eating oatmeal.

So, sometime in the morning, the day and time not being in my range of knowledge, because paying attention to time is like counting atoms, and also, I wasn't wearing a watch.

Then, of course, as I am sure you have guessed (all this building up had to be going somewhere), The Big Thing happened.

Surprise, surprise, I know.

And here is how It happened, or at least how I remember it.

As I sat in my cave, looking out my entrance to the entrance of the pyramid, through the haze of the heat, I suddenly saw four figures, seemingly appear from nowhere, walking towards the entrance to the Pyramid.

Now, here, there are two problems. One, I had not actually gotten in to the pyramid. I couldn't solve the rather intricate code, glyphs, and puzzle on the door, as one, it was nothing like anything I had seen before, and two, because I hadn't had much time after dark.

So, since whoever was going to the pyramid obviously knew it was there (you could see nothing of it but the well-hidden door), and they obviously had been there before, because they were through the door as fast as you or I could open our own front door.

Now, all the Creatures in It All have faults. We are all dumb in one way or another. Many of us, of course, have more faults than others.

At first, I thought for certain that Humans had entered the front door because they left it wide open after they entered.

I came running, wanting to:

A) see who it was, and

B) ask them about the door-code, just out of curiosity. What I found afterward was nothing short of…fairly boring. A long tunnel led deep underground. Of course. Now, I had made it to the door less than a minute after it had opened, and the odd thing was that there were no lights to be seen in the tunnel. I could hear no footfalls, see no lights of lamps or torches, hear no speech.

Fast little bastards, I thought.

In my excitement, I had of course forgotten my torch, and decided there was no time for it anyway. I started off down the tunnel.

I felt my way down the tunnel, and after about a hundred meters, the tunnel took a hard right. I continued to follow, and found a hard left after about twenty more meters. So the speed of the visitors disappearance was explained, in a manner of speaking. Now, I saw the sort of thing that adventurers and observers live for. A faint green light, at about a 20 degree angle, about 100 meters away.

I sped down the tunnel, with no regard for traps, holes, or other such hazards, and soon came to the opening.

Now, I am not usually a complete fool. Usually. But today, in my excitement, I was more than a fool. I burst around the last corner into a large cavern, and came face-to-face with my predecessors.

They were surprised, to say the least.

Now, I have to say, until this point, I had only had experience with Creatures of Earth. I had never seen anything remotely Alien.

These were undoubtedly Aliens.

That's a pretty big Something.

Now, these were not little green men, not big scary monster Aliens, but there was no doubt about their Alien-ness.

It wasn't so much that I remember them looking like anything special, it was just that they seemed to know everything they needed within seconds of seeing me come around the corner. It was almost like looking at them made you lose your ability to recall what anything else looked like, so there was no way that you could make comparisons. But all the same, beautiful beyond all thought, bringing to mind the most beautiful thing you have ever laid eyes on, but not being able to recall what exactly that thing was.

Disconcerting, especially for one so adept at observing.

Now, not to my surprise (nor to yours, I am sure), I was immediately disregarded as a threat. It wasn't that they told me this, it was just that, after my grand entrance, they just went on about their business, as if I wasn't there, or couldn't do anything about anything, even if I was there. I suddenly felt like a small child in a room of adults. I stood there like a little fool, and spoke the best thing I could think of.

"Hello?"

Then, to my dismay, I was spoken to, in my language, not in my mind, not quite telepathically, but certainly louder and bigger than you could expect from a seemingly un-amplified voice.

"Yes, we see you there, now, go run and play, we have work to do."

Now, being an adult, albeit a younger one, not to mention one who considered himself wise well beyond his years, this came as a slap in the person. To be treated like a child!

So I did the best thing I could think of.

I acted like a child.

"Who are You! What are You? Where are You from? How did You get here? What are You doing?"

Silence, and a pause.

Then one of the Creatures approached me, and, exactly as an adult would to a child, spoke softer, but yet still louder than you or I could. Think of pressing headphones against your ears as you listen to loud music. Like that.

"Don't worry…we are here to help."

Then another of them spoke.

"Bob, don't waste your time over there, we have things to do here."

And then a third.

"I knew we should have been a little more careful."

The first one again.

"Well, we might as well try to explain, that It is here at all is a bit of an accomplishment, and furthermore, he probably won't leave us alone until we do something of the sort. They are like that, you know."

"True, but try to make it quick, and then make him sit still and behave."

The creature turned back to me, and right as it was about to speak, its eyes fell to my left hand.

In all my excitement, I had forgotten all about my oatmeal. I still held the bowl in my hand.

Now, you would think a Creature as seemingly amazing as these would have heard of oatmeal, and certainly had 15,000 different varieties from the seven corners of the Galaxy.

You'd be wrong.

CHAPTER 8
SOMEONE ELSE'S TURN

In another place, at another time, Joe Goodman sat at breakfast, eating some oatmeal. He didn't usually have oatmeal for breakfast, but that didn't cross his mind at the moment.

He had all sorts of breakfast cereals.

Joe was a larger fellow, not fat, not slim, not short, not inordinately tall, but larger than average. He was younger looking, and there was nothing about him that would cause you to pause and wonder at his presence. He would get your attention if he wanted it.

The most amazing thing about Joe was that he was an Alien.

And he didn't know it.

Oh, there were clues, obviously. He had an incredible ability to manipulate, and an incredible ability for observing.

In my experience, the former almost always follows the latter.

He was not one to overuse his powers, although he did use them. Then there were the other things. The ability exist on nearly no sleep was one, and then the yet undiscovered ability to fly.

Joe couldn't fly yet because he was all-too-interested in Human mathematics. Human mathematics have various rules and regulations, one of which is that Humans cannot fly without mechanical aid. There are numerous other planets, in our own Galaxy, let alone Universe, where it is common knowledge that all Humanoids, and all sentient Creatures, for that matter, can fly, if they want to. The first and main thing they have to either know nothing about, or more importantly, care nothing about, mathematics.

One of the best examples is dolphins.

Back to Joe. Joe was Alien. Joe was very like you and any other Humans you might know, in the physiological, and biological sense. He was an oxygen-breathing, carbon-based Being. That he happened to be born on another planet, and one not-at-all that distant from ours, scarcely changes that. Were Joe to ever be incredibly sick (a near impossibility), or, perhaps, be subjected to a thorough DNA examination, it may have been recognized that his makeup was ever-so-slightly different. He would also live just about 40% longer than you might.

The next question was how Joe got here.

Joe was deposited on Earth as punishment.

Now, I know what you are thinking. Earth is not that bad. It is not a terrible prison, where all planets of the surrounding solar systems send their criminals, and so on and so forth. You'd be right to a certain extent. Joe was not a criminal. He was a good Being, and was deposited here, memory wiped, because he had spoken too loudly on his own planet. Not about anything, or against anything. He had literally spoken too loudly on his old planet.

Volume-wise.

Where Joe came from, they had silly laws, just like Earth does. Earth has silly laws governing, for instance, what you can—and cannot—eat, drink, smoke, or otherwise consume. On Joe's old planet, you could consume anything you wanted, you just had to be quiet about it. If you wanted to be loud, you had to do it in the privacy of your own, well sound-proofed home, and even then, you could be reported and turned in, imprisoned even.

Joe found this as ludicrous as you or I might. He started a revolt, and got quite a few people speaking above a whisper. The thing about Joe was that his observation and manipulation talents are not inherited, or inherent, for that matter, because he was an Alien, anymore than your talents are inherent because you breathe air.

So, it's not so much that They, The People That Run Things, on Joe's planet thought that Earth was sufficiently terrible a punishment, it was just that they found it sufficiently loud.

Joe remembered nothing of this, of course.

At least for the moment.

So, Joe was eating some oatmeal, in his house, on the beach. Minding his own business, if for no other reason, Joe lived on his own island. How he obtained his island is not really important, although I am sure you can begin to guess at the strength of Joe's powers since he had his own island. His island was in the middle of the ocean, of course, and maybe more importantly, the Pacific Ocean. It was nearly 50 miles to the nearest island, and 100 miles from any real civilization.

A place where Joe could be as loud as he liked, and often was.

At this place, at this time, there was a noise outside that could not have been ignored.

A huge, rumbling, whining howl that approached the island at incredible speed. Joe sprang from his hut, turned to the noise, and saw an object, purple and silver...what could you call it?

Nothing, but nothing, was ever more spaceship.

A pretty big Something.

And we are not talking flying saucer, but we are talking the most impossibly gaudy piece of purple and silver space hotrod ever. Neon running lights, in 17 colors, lightning bolts, and we aren't talking painted on, we are talking actual electrical currents, from front to back, and seven boosters, each the size of garbage cans. The ship itself was maybe only ten meters long, and it certainly was an impressive sight.

Joe stood aghast.

The ship landed on a small hill maybe 20 meters from Joe's hut. The noise subsided almost as quickly as it had come.

A ramp lowered itself from the belly of the craft, and out walked what disappointingly looked like a Human. It walked towards Joe, a medium height, medium build, brown haired, young...man. He was wearing a dirty t-shirt, covered with a flannel button down, jeans, and sandals. Large, yellow, rhinestone aviator glasses covered his eyes.

He loudly called out to Joe.

"GREETINGS, CREATURE OF THE GALAXY! SORRY TO INTRUDE! CAME INTO THE ATMOSPHERE IN THE WRONG PLACE I GUESS!"

Joe started to open his mouth to speak, but the young man interrupted him.

"Like my ride there? Yeah, that is suh-suh-wheet, huh? Hey, you got anything to eat? I'm starving."

Joe finally found his ability to speak, and found that he was still holding his breakfast in his hand.

"I have some…oatmeal here."

"Oatmeal, huh? Never heard of it. Let me give it a whack-a-dilly."

The young man took the bowl, and using his fingers, took a scoop and a bite.

"Not bad…not bad at all! Hey, mind if we go inside and sit down? Do you drink? Like water? I see you've got lots of it. By the way, my name is Anthony. I'm a musician."

He held out his hand, after wiping it on his pant-leg. Joe took it, without really thinking, and shook Anthony's hand.

"I'm…my name is Joe."

"Well, hey there Joe…nice to meet 'cha. Um. Well, I don't mean to pry, but did you know that you have some blockage?"

"Excuse me?"

"Some blockage. Brain Blockage. Here, let me get that for you."

And as quick as you can say "peanut," he reached out and slapped Joe right upside the head.

And Joe remembered everything.

CHAPTER 9
HANDSHAKES

Most people don't know this, but shaking hands/fins/flippers/paws/tentacles/whatever-else-you-may-have is the Standard Greeting among all Creatures in all the known places in the entire Galaxy. And actually, in the entire known Universe. Beyond that, nobody knows. How this started or how it was spread or when it was started or when it spread, or how long it has been around, nobody knows that either.

The funny thing is that it's not the standard on Earth. There have been wars fought over proper greetings, I am sure.

Where Anthony Seven-Two-Three-Nine was from, handshakes were the norm. In fact, it was the first thing you learned how to do. You didn't say "Mama" or "Dada," as you didn't have one. On Anthony's planet, directly on the other side of the Milky Way, you were made to order, in accordance with the current population of the planet. It was always kept at equilibrium. You were given a first name at random, and then your "last name" was just in accordance with how many "Bobs" or "Johns" there were before you. Then, the entire community was responsible for raising you. You grew up and were educated among your peers.

This concept might strike a Human as odd, even immoral. However, the only thing predetermined was that you were to have no genetic diseases or disorders. Everything else was randomly selected. There were no supermen, no invalids. Just as much diversity as any other planet in color of hair, skin, eyes, etc.

People from Anthony's planet looked like Humans, as do many of the Aliens of the Galaxy.

They were, however, much more advanced. Interstellar transportation was as old as anyone could remember, and people lived to be 300 years old. Or more.

And they were telepathic.

It may or may not have been a genetic "defect" that was discovered and decided upon as beneficial, but it had happened much to long ago for anyone to remember. It had advanced to the point where people from Anthony's planet could manipulate people, or help them, depending on their mood.

This might strike you as very bad.

To Humans, it certainly could be. If the others of Anthony's type were hostile, or evil, or anywhere close to Earth, it certainly could have been pretty bad. However, none of these were the case.

Besides, most Creatures have ways of keeping people out of their minds. Furthermore, most Creatures have, at the very least, a latent telepathic ability.

Humans, however, are not "Most Creatures."

Back to Anthony.

Anthony was as far from a hostile, menacing, Alien as you could get. When he used his tellies (Common Galactic for telepathic powers) it was usually only to soothe the effects of meeting an Alien, or for removing brainwashing, or tellie blocks and additions.

He was a nice Alien.

He was also a musician. He played the several instruments, all of Alien design, but he also played what we call the guitar. It wasn't that it was a different from our guitars, in fact, it was one of our guitars.

In order for this to be explained, you have to understand that Earth is an anomaly in this Galaxy. Now, what I would technically find out later, and you will find out now, is that Everyone knows about us, and we know about Nobody. We are really the only Planet with any sort of civilization that hasn't learned Interstellar Travel, or how to get along.

We are a curiosity.

Some planets say it is because We are young, which, as a Civilization, We are. Others, not much older than Us, say We are just plain stupid.

It's a matter of much debate.

So, now-needless-to-say, Earth Objects are a curiosity and highly collectible.

And Anthony had a guitar.

And, by our standards, he was very good at it. This came as no surprise to Anthony, as he had been randomly pre-dispositioned to be a talented musician. Now, on Anthony's planet, you are not told, as a rule, what you are pre-dispositioned to be or do. You must find out for yourself. Some would have many talents, some only one.

But Everyone had one.

As a rule.

So Anthony could play the guitar. And he was coming to Earth to do just that.

In many places, for many reasons, it was not "cool" to play the guitar, or any Earth instrument for that matter. Most of them were considered too simple, for one. The only exception was the piano. Almost every planet had a version. And pianos of Earth were highly valued. Seemed that no one could make a piano like a Human.

How else, but for Aliens buying them, do you think that the Grand Piano Business is kept in business?

Not that many Humans play the piano.

But Anthony loved the guitar. And the only place he could do that and be appreciated, really appreciated, was Earth.

He was going to be a rock star.

The fact that he had accidentally entered Earth's atmosphere in the middle of the ocean, rather than the mountain range he had planned on was not a real surprise, or a real problem for Anthony.

He was an easygoing guy.

He was also approaching his 120th birthday, which you couldn't tell by looking at him, or listening to him, for that matter.

The fact that this stranger had occupied the first small island he found was something of interest, especially since it was so far from anything.

Even more interesting was that the Creature occupying the island was an Alien.

A brainwashed Alien.

Then, last but not least, there was the strange substance he had been eating and offered to Anthony. Ohtmeal? It was delicious, and Anthony had never heard of it.

The funny thing is, no Alien had. In all their meddling and watching and collecting, few Aliens were so brave to eat Human food. Those that did ate things that seemed interesting.

Oatmeal, as you know, is not that interesting.

So, Anthony, not being one prone to rudeness, or one to pass up free food, gave it a "wack-a-dilly."

And he thoroughly enjoyed it.

Needless to say, this would come in handy for both Anthony and Joe (not to mention Humanity) later on.

CHAPTER 10
ANOTHER TIME, ANOTHER PLACE

Somewhere, in another time, in another place…Dan Wright was sitting over his desk, studying. It was a common occurrence, as he was studying to be a doctor, which someday would make him Dr. Wright. He was already Mr. Wright. He liked being Wright.

You'd want him studying.

Dan was of medium height, well built, blonde hair, blue eyes. He worked out and ate well. He was, as it were, completely Human.

He also ate a lot of oatmeal.

In fact, it was almost absurd how much he ate oatmeal. He ate if for its low-fat goodness and for its fiber. He bought it in huge boxes at a local wholesaler. He ate it plain. Dan didn't know this, and never would, but he ate more oatmeal than any other person on the planet.

Which, in a weird way, is quite the accomplishment.

Dan also didn't know that his oatmeal eating habits would, on that very day, involve him in an Intergalactic incident.

Dan had many traits, good and bad, just like everyone, but one of the stand out traits was Dan was very organized. He was really organized. Really what I am trying to say is he was anal-retentive to the point of obsessive-compulsive. But in a good way.

Everything had its place. Not to the millimeter or anything, but certainly, the same place every time.

There was something funny about the way things were at Dan's on this particular day.

There was no oatmeal.

This didn't usually happen. When the supply started to run low, Dan went out and bought more boxes of oatmeal and thus the supply was restocked. And it was unlike him that he hadn't done so.

Was he slipping?

Maybe the three tests a week and the whole learning every-little-thing-about-the-Human-body thing had him distracted.

You'd want him distracted.

So, he put it on his To Do list. Which he took ten minutes to type out every day.

Later that day, he went to the store to get a few things, including but not limited to oatmeal. As he left the store, it was just past 11 p.m. in his time zone, and dark. He hopped in his car and started back to his apartment.

Now, here is another good point to make. Dan loved his car. It was a nice car, and a fast one, and if you haven't noticed, that is the kind of car all doctors have. He was still just a medical student, but he would be a doctor soon enough.

No reason not to have the car now.

Furthermore, Dan liked to drive his fast car fast. What else was it fast for? And, as it was dark, and late, there was no reason whatsoever not to drive fast.

Now is a good time to talk about doctors. Maybe "doctors" isn't necessarily the best term, but it's the Human term, and in our scope, it makes sense. Caretakers, Healers, Health Helpers...those are all terms used by Aliens.

Aliens think Human doctors are funny. First, they are a little behind the Galactic measure of medicine. Second, they only have two different anatomies to deal with, and they are not that drastically different. Most Alien "doctors" have at least twice that, and more often than not, they are drastically different.

There is one certainty, though. Human doctors get paid much, much more than any Alien doctors.

Now, this doesn't mean much on a Galactic scale, as our money means nothing anywhere, except as a novelty. The rest of the Galaxy has been on the Candus Credit for the last 10,000 years.

Some Aliens doctors are perturbed by the fact that, per capita, Human doctors are paid so well. So much in fact, that many of them give up Galactic Medicine and come to live on Earth. It's just that on Earth, doctors are paid lots of money to be good. And rich. In the rest of the Galaxy, doctors are paid to be doctors, and forced to be good. There are several sectors where simple misdiagnosis results in severe punishment. Those, of course, are the harsher sectors.

Now, certainly, there are many Earth doctors who are doctors to help people. Maybe even the majority of them. But there are quite a few who are just in it for the money.

However, this was not the case with the Character we are discussing now. He eventually wanted to be a good doctor, and help people.

So, going faster than the allotted speed on a road he knew very well, later in the evening, with no cars out and about, you could imagine Dan's surprise when he nearly hit a spaceship.

Now, in normal traffic situations, a car, a truck, a bus, a semi-tractor carrying a house, whatever, Dan would have been able to avoid the accident. He was a good driver.

But this was a spaceship. It just came out of nowhere. And it's not that Dan did or did not believe in spaceships, and aliens, and other such extraterrestrial things, it was more that he didn't spend that much time thinking about that particular subject.

You wouldn't want him thinking about that sort of thing. You'd want him thinking about where all your parts are, and how to fix them if and when they break.

So Dan went off the road and hit several of the trees that were so thoughtlessly placed by the road. And this might have made him angry if he wasn't knocked unconscious. The only thing he could remember was spaceship, trees, dark.

And the only thing you should remember is that Dan had a trunk full of oatmeal.

CHAPTER 11
LONG (OR TALL) AND SHORT OF IT

Tony and Neil were an odd pair. Tony, as you may remember, is an Alien. Neil is half Human, and half Alien. (There have been several Alien/Human matings over the years.) The interesting part, I think, is that they are, technically, half brothers. (Same father, different mothers.)

A cosmic soap-opera, as you can see.

First, if you were to see Tony and Neil, you would see that they were physically quite different. Neil was well over six feet tall, and Tony was well under. Neil was skinny, Tony was stocky. Neil had light hair, but not blond, and Tony had dark hair, but not black.

Neil knew he was half-Human but hardly claimed it, and Tony knew he was all Alien, and didn't flaunt it.

The Galaxial equivalent of Mutt and Jeff.

Or perhaps something more. Tony and Neil, or Neil and Tony, depending on who you talked to, were Extremely Famous.

Now, of course, you have never heard of them, because you are most likely a Human. And Humans are not often privy to the Who's Who list of the Galaxy.

See, it is one thing to be famous on a Planet. Then other to be famous in a sector, or a quadrant. But Neil and Tony, or Tony and Neil, depending on who you talked to, were famous in several Galaxies.

Neil and Tony (we'll stick with alphabetical order for this chapter, so we don't have to keep depending on people) weren't famous for things that people are famous on Earth for. They weren't famous actors, or musicians, or scientists, although, technically, they were all of these things.

Nor were they famous for something silly like being good at throwing a ball around, or being able to hit a fellow Being in some manner or another.

No, Neil and Tony were absurdly, disgustingly, Extremely Famous quite simply because they were two of the Coolest Beings in The Milky Way.

This was their actual title. How you come or go about getting this title is rather obscure.

There are no tests taken, no deeds done. You just become one of the Coolest Beings in the Galaxy. No one really knows who decides these things either. There are a couple hundred of them, but out of quadrillions of Beings, it's a short list.

And in being one of the Coolest Beings in the Galaxy really opens up doors. You can be a musician even if you aren't any good at all, be an actor if you deliver lines like a peanut, and get free drinks just about anywhere.

However, this never happens. All of the Coolest Beings in the Galaxy are good at whatever they do. There was the one exception of the Suruvian who was given Coolest Being in the Galaxy status simply because he was absolutely the largest dork to ever live.

He couldn't do anything right.

It wasn't that Tony and Neil were the same in personality, either. In fact, they were very different. Well, different in a base sense. Imagine two puzzles made from the same die…the pieces are all the same, but the pictures are different.

Really, the Truth was, that Neil and Tony just got along really really well. They had not once in the entire time they had known each other, had a fight. They even seldom disagreed, and when they did, they just agreed to disagree.

Some very amiable fellows, as you can see.

So, Neil and Tony were Extremely Famous.

And they spent most of their time wandering the Galaxy partying it up.

One of their favorite party spots was a bar on one of the ends of one of the arms of the Milky Way. Named the Atomic Cat, for reasons best not discussed in pleasant company, it was one of the "Places to Be" in the Milky Way, and was listed on the Top Ten Coolest Bars Named after Irradiated Animals (you'd be surprised how many there are) in Universal Life Magazine.

The Atomic Cat was owned and operated by a six-armed sage bartender named Justin, who, if you were paying attention earlier, you know gives strangely relevant advice at crucial moments.

And so there, their story begins within our Story.

It was one of those "drunken" things. You know the type. Bar conversation. And it always sounds so good when you are there.

And, for some reason, it just never is.

Neil and Tony had been out doing that thing they did (which, for the moment, was nothing more than mooching, but they got away with it.) and had finally ended up at the Atomic Cat, where they could always get their drinks for free.

Now, a departure must be taken here to explain something. Across the Galaxy, there are three things that absolutely do not change. All the advanced technologies, knowledge, and general common sense could not change them. Eons of experience, light years of research. Constants.

Smoking, drinking, and sex.

Every Culture, every Civilization, every World, every Species has some form of these or another. Certainly, there are those who abstain for various reasons. Brain, liver, general body damage. Hangovers. Vomiting. Addiction. In many alien cultures, it became so prevalent, so problematic, that the different scientific communities directed all efforts on not preventing these ailments, but curing them.

So, it is suffice to say that the rest of the Galaxy can get sloshed, smoked, wasted, washed, seven-sheets-to-the-wind drunk, high as a kite, smoke like smokestacks, and hump anything that moves without worrying about a single tumor; lump; red spot; hangover; virus; liver, kidney, lung, or brain cell.

There is a fascination with the Human dilemma on these subjects. Aliens find it quite humorous that our skewed sense of morality has not only kept medicine from advancing on these territories, but has kept society from advancing on these territories.

So, while the rest of the Galaxy gets drunk, high, and laid with no consequences...we still have to "face that morning music," as they say.

Back to Neil and Tony.

Now, by this point, Neil and Tony had been drinking for about 3 weeks. Not just at night, but all day, every day. Their state of drunkenness had waxed and waned, but now, now was the full harvest moon of their drunkenness.

And it was Tony who said, in that bar talk...

"You know what would be funny? We should go visit Earth."

And Neil replied...

"Hey, yeah...that would be fun."

And Justin, the six-armed sage bartender who gives relevant advice at crucial moments said simply...

"That's not a very good idea."

Needless to say, like so many bartenders since the dawn of time, on every Planet, Justin was wholly ignored.

And 15 minutes later, Neil and Tony were running into a very specific person, at a very specific place, at a very specific time. As his very fast white car ran off the road and hit a tree...Neil and Tony looked at each other, dazed, confused, drunk as skunks, and said together...

"Aw...shit."

CHAPTER 12
ON WORDS AND WARRIORS

Another thing that is quite constant throughout the Galaxy is cursing. No amount of advancement, no amount of intelligence, no endless centuries of evolution and cultural growth can change the fact that sometimes, Sentient Creatures need to emphasize.

And of course, like so many things derived from Conscience Beings...there is a pattern. Swearing, almost without fail, falls into three categories. Scatological, Sex Oriented, or Familial Insults.

Certainly, there are variations...but these are the main categories. Others include Animal Body Parts, Animals in General, and Insults based on level of intelligence.

And there are those in the Galaxy, certainly, who do not curse in any form. Generally, the view is those who don't ever curse are not to be trusted. There are exceptions. Sometimes those who don't curse are simply feared.

Which brings us to Josh. When I say the word/name Josh, you might think of several people, or characters, or friends from the past. And you and I might even think of the same "famous" people here on

Earth. Everyone else in the Galaxy did something similar. The name Josh, anywhere in the Milky Way, quite literally conjures the same image, same stories, and same terror in every single Being. Except, of course, on Earth.

Whether this helps or harms us is yet to be seen.

Josh was the Premiere of the Intergalactic Police. Now, while this would normally bring to mind an aging, fatting, politician behind a desk, and certainly used to, now, the position carried the weight that can only be carried by fear.

Josh grew up in an Intergalactic Police family. His father was a Commander. He went to the Intergalactic Police Academy. While this might sound like a terrible movie, it was actually a training program that would put the toughest Special Forces men on Earth to tears. Needless to say, there wasn't an Earth policeman alive that could have completed it.

He graduated with flying colors, top of his class, and then went on to become a Commander, just like his father. His unique style and finesse quickly catapulted him to the top of his Sector, then Quadrant, then soon, the Galaxy. After this his "political" rise to Premiere was simply a matter of time. At 212, he became the youngest Premiere in the history of the Intergalactic Police (which was well over 20,000 years old.)

Usually, and hopefully, this would have, and was supposed to, end his Tours. But, instead, it increased them. He would not sit behind the desk and orchestrate, no, he had to be in the field. He would have been removed, had he not been so damn good.

Now, in the Galaxy called the Milky Way, the laws were very simple. Lawyers as we know them had been done away with millennia ago. There were four very simple rules. And they were written as such.

The Universal Codified Law Of the Milky Way:

1. Don't kill people without cause.

2. Don't take things that aren't yours.

3. Be nice to others.

4. Don't mess with other planets/civilizations/cultures.

Now, while these may seem arbitrary, and generally, terribly open to interpretation, and let's not forget that they are, these four rules had generally been keeping the peace for 20,000 years. The Intergalactic Police were the Pursuants, Judges, and Juries on these laws.

You might think that these simple laws are not enough to run a Galaxy, but you would be wrong for the most part. Certainly people would do things that seemingly fell outside of these rules, but a connection could always be made.

Of course, each planet has their own laws, some of them, just variations on a theme, others with rule sets that make Earth tax laws look simple.

And punishment? Usually imprisonment. You would be sent to a work camp, or locked in a tiny cell. Also, depending on your infraction, and your resistance to capture, you might just be vaporized. Humans who think of themselves as "enlightened" with knowledge of the "sanctity of life" might cringe a bit at this, but the rest of the Galaxy is beyond such silliness. They know damn well that vaporizing a person just redistributes their energy, and that sometimes it is just necessary. What about the innocents? Well, it should be known that very few people are actually innocent. Innocent of a particular, yes, but totally innocent? Not likely. Also, part of the very basic training in the Intergalactic Police Academy is telepathy. If an Intergalactic Policeman just happens to vaporize the wrong person for the wrong reason, he will know it, and so will any other telepaths. And then he would be removed from the very honorable position, and probably imprisoned or vaporized. It's been known to happen.

Also, if you happen to shoot at an Intergalactic Policeman?

Yeah. Vaporized.

Now, you might be thinking, "What about all this talk of the Universe and Galaxy as this, advanced, supreme, peaceful society?"

You have to remember, nobody's perfect.

There is still crime, there are still wars, there are still power struggles, because that is the nature of being conscious. But we are talking about more creatures than you can possibly imagine, and per capita, the crime rate is so low that it is almost indecipherable, but still, there are millions of crimes committed every day.

Not all Creatures are that far past us in social terms. Just general knowledge, scientific knowledge, Universal knowledge, etc.

Back to Josh.

Josh was, to use a title, the best of the best. If you committed a crime that came to his attention, you had better watch out. Or really, you probably just ought to turn yourself in, because Josh always got his man/woman/asexual being.

The biggest, and strangest, of all these things was that while Josh was quite possibly the most feared being in the Galaxy, a menacing sight, and as bad-ass as they come, he was really a very nice guy. You just didn't want to break the law around him, that was all.

The truth of the matter is, you, regardless if you want to or not, should appreciate, respect, and thank Josh.

He's saved you from destruction on several occasions.

You see, there are definitely those that would destroy Earth. Why, you ask? For the same reason that the Intergalactic Police go out of their way to protect us. Earth is an anomaly. We stand out. Just like everyone knows about Josh, everyone knows about Earth. We are the center of huge debates, and much conversation. We are ridiculed and we are lambasted as nothing more than slime. We are also praised as artifacts, and as interesting reading. However, it is the Intergalactic Police's business to protect Sentient Beings.

Josh himself had taken a peculiar interest in Earth, as had his father. He actually kept an Earth Creature as a pet. He had a kitten. He had acquired it from a Grand Piano smugglers ship, and kept it in his office. He fed it Hurugian Kelp Fish, and it soothed him. Such a small creature, so fragile, yet so fearless...he admired that.

So, somewhat thanks to a feline ball of fur, we are somewhat safe.

As you will soon see, not as safe as you would like to be.

CHAPTER 13
ON TRUTH AND WRITERS

There is an old saying. The Truth hurts.

People say this because it is true.

It is also the reason that most people don't have the slightest idea about what is the Truth and what is not. Most go slip sliding on through, creating comfortable realities. People are always saying that the Truth is elusive. That's silly. The truth is that Truth is the opposite of elusive. It is usually right there, staring you in the face, it is just a matter of whether or not you want to accept it.

Now certainly, there is plenty that is not Truth. There is even more proposing to be the Truth, which is not. Furthermore, there is plenty speculated to be the Truth, when really, speculation and revelation, as far as finding the Truth goes, are about as handy as a bouncy ball.

It's always what you think you know.

Some people have a knack for the Truth, and others have a propensity for avoiding it. Our next Character is one of the former bent. Terry Vrais is a writer. He is a Human, but, an inHuman one. Not in the sense that he drop-kicks kittens, but rather that he has an inHuman ability.

He can always find the Truth.

Needless to say, this has driven him to drink.

Terry once was a writer for a very famous and well-regarded newspaper. The kind of newspaper that prides itself in telling the Truth, the real news, with no bias. Of course, anyone with a drop of common sense knows that this is more or less impossible. And, since there are very few with a drop of common sense, this paper sold millions of copies to even more readers.

One day, well after the beginning of his job, Terry was struck with a Sense of Truth. This is a common affliction, almost like a virus, that is known throughout the Universe. Most Aliens get vaccinated against it, for the simple fact that they don't want to deal with it.

How it happens is more or less a mystery, but we do know that it happens in times of high stress.

Terry had stress.

Not only did he live in New York City, and Manhattan at that, he was a writer for a major newspaper. To top all that off, he had lots of money.

Most people don't know it, but having lots of money is the Number One cause of stress.

Not to mention that he had a girlfriend. And not just any girlfriend, but a heinous bitch of a girlfriend. She left.

Sometimes that's all it takes.

So, now Terry has lots of stress, and lots of money, which he spends on very expensive fermented grapes, on which he gets very expensively drunk.

One night, during a specifically bad time, Terry jumped into the bathtub, on his second bottle of very expensive fermented grapes. When he woke up, the water was red with his very expensive fermented grapes, and it hit him.

"That was stupid."

And the truth hurt, and badly enough to give Terry's brain that whack necessary to take it to the next level.

Now he could see the Truth.

So, he wrote it in his next article. The Truth. Bald and Beautiful. No holds barred. And through some favors pulled, it went to press, instead of making it's usual stop at the editor's desk. The editor got and approved the story Terry had originally written which was only speckled with the Truth.

So, the Truth was out.

And no one gave a shit.

Almost no one.

The story rolled…Terry was fired, and the world had no idea what had happened. There was the Truth, plain and simple, staring them in the face. It was, of course passed off as the ranting of a cracked man, which was, for the most part, correct. It doesn't change that it was the Truth.

The story more or less disintegrated.

So now Terry was out of a job, out of his nice apartment, and nice fermented grapes, out of a girlfriend.

The upside was that he didn't care, because he had the Truth.

Now, it needs to be pointed out that while Terry had the Truth, he did not have the Whole Truth. That would have killed him. (The Whole Truth has taken many lives throughout the Universe. That's why we don't know what the Whole Truth actually is. Anyone who finds it dies.) No, Terry just had portions of the Truth. There were a few things that he knew.

1. Life does not end at death.

2. What you know, rather than what you have, is all that is important.

3. There are Aliens.

Incidentally, the second of the three was what caused the most discourse. Apparently, most people believe in Aliens, but not diminishing their capitalism.

Pretty standard, really.

So, now that Terry had the Partial Truth, his problems all but disappeared. For the moment. The thing is, knowing there are Aliens and actually meeting one are two completely different propositions. And Terry was about to run into the latter of the two propositions sooner than he probably would have liked.

Before we go on…two things.

One. You need to remember that Terry still has lots of money. Going "crazy" didn't evaporate his assets. He more or less evaporated his assets into a large chunk of change. Sold his stocks, his bonds, his car, all of his things. He kept some cloths, his laptop, and of course, his money.

Two. Sometimes the search for knowledge is expensive, so let's not judge here.

Now, I suppose you think that Terry is going to meet an alien, over a bowl of oatmeal, but you'd be wrong. The Story is not that predictable. No, Terry is about to meet another Human…one who will help him on his search for knowledge…and most importantly, one who believes him.

CHAPTER 14
CAPITALIST PIGS

Greg Van Heusan was a capitalist pig. He made lots of money, more or less doing nothing. Greg was the guy that walked into a room, a room of people who showed him something, and he would say, "Yes, no, do this, don't do that." Then, "Where's my check?"

This is not even remotely to say that Greg was a bad person. He was not. By most standards, he was a good person. (The standards not included here are most religious standards, by which everyone will die and burn in a very bad place.) He donated time and money to those who had less than he, he did not litter, he was more or less kind to those who passed by him in his life.

Greg had his faults, like everyone else. One of his faults was that he was incredibly intelligent, and he knew it. No one likes a person who knows they are smart.

It's apparently very annoying.

Greg was also very cynical…and you already knew this, if you had been paying attention earlier.

Greg's largest fault was his lack of faith in mankind. Like so many before and after him, he didn't think most people could make the cut under their own power. He figured that he had it figured out, and he let people know what he had figured out.

And they paid him for it.

Combine this with a incredible money sense, a few very good investments, a proclivity for (fairly) simple living, and you have yourself a very rich young man.

Greg was a self-made man with an old money name and all-new money.

He was also 27, and several times a millionaire.

You can imagine the problems when the 27-year-old walks into your office, tells you and the rest of your 50 to 60-year-old board members how to do it right…and have him be right.

Trouble all around.

Which brings us to the real problem. Greg was always right. It has nothing to do with the fact that he "thought" he was always right…no, he was actually always right.

Disagreeing with him was difficult, and arguing? Forget about it.

Greg actually did as well a job as one could do about concealing the fact that he knew he was always right.

As well as one could, I suppose.

It wasn't just that Greg was right about business strategy, or politics, or money issues…he was also always right about people.

It needs to be pointed out, however, that always being right was not the same as knowing the Truth.

There were other things about Greg, both good and bad, which is the case with everyone, of course. He had a tendency towards impatience and perfectionism, and therefore egomania and elitism. These are things that you loved right away about Greg, or never really quite got used to.

He had an interesting family life, not to say bad, not to say good. Good parents, nice siblings...he called on holidays and birthdays, but there was something about Greg that kept him separated from everyone.

It's not that he didn't have friends, and it's not that he didn't have good friends. It's that there was always something that put him on the outside looking in. No one else noticed it, but Greg always knew. There was something bigger out there. Bigger than him, bigger than anything anyone had ever known. He just had that feeling, that would set him aside at a party in reflection and observation, rather than joining in. A feeling that kept him awake, not in fear or longing, but just awake and thinking. It had been with him his whole life.

Which brings us to our way point.

The point where Greg Van Heusan meets Terry Vrais, in case you weren't paying attention again.

Greg got up, as he always did, at 6:56 a.m. Greg only set his clock so the numbers were the same forwards and backwards.

He didn't really even know why.

Greg was a very scheduled person. This is not to say that he never strayed from his schedule, as he was a fairly adventurous person.

However, when he was not being adventurous, he had a schedule that he kept out of habit rather than necessity.

After he got up, he would go get the paper that was laid in front of the door in his very nice, albeit modest for a multimillionaire, Manhattan condo. Greg was actually one of those people whose money did not cause him stress. The reason for this was since he was always right, he always knew what to do and what not to do with his money.

Then, he would go sit down at his kitchen table, and read the paper over a cup of coffee, oatmeal, and some toast. Whole wheat toast.

Because it's better for you.

Greg did not look like your typical consultant/entrepreneur, if there is such a thing.

He did not look like either the thin, graying, professional entrepreneur, nor the slick, styled, motivational-speaker-look of the consultant. Nor was he of the new wave of young millionaires, looking frumpy and silly in their wrinkled $2,000 suits and t-shirts, complete with vintage sneakers. He looked like a normal person. He had wire-rim glasses, was not all that tall, and had a Buddha belly. He wore nice clothes that he had made for him, but not expensively. He wore a chain watch, and was usually found in a vest.

You might think he was a banker, from the 1940s, lost in time.

Today, however, something quite different happened. When he picked up the paper, he turned to the editorial page, and went right to his favorite columnist.

You might have guessed whom already.

As he began to read the article, he realized something was different. The tone was heavier, the subject, rather than the usual humorous social commentary or condemnation to a manifesto of sorts. Then it began to dawn on him what he was reading.

The Truth.

Greg finished the article, put down the paper, and picked up his phone.

CHAPTER 15
THE CHILD INSIDE

Isabella was a strange child. It's not that she looked any different that a small child, or really acted that much differently from her peers. It was small, and mostly unobserved, instances that set her apart.

Flashes of insight.

In everyone's mind, things come in very random patterns, as you may have forgotten, in a child's mind, unlike when you are older, these patterns are not yet recognizable. As you get older, you learn to parse these patterns into phenomenon that you place a name to. Smells, sights, tastes, sounds, textures. It is patterns of thought, of mental images projected from others that either you never learn to combine into the tangible, or it takes years of practice to develop.

A Sixth Sense.

Of course, the rest of the Universe knows there are actually Seven Senses, and we know it, too, but most of us have forgotten or never knew how to use that particular seventh power.

Isabella was different in this regard.

She was going on 3, and had been an only child raised in a strange family. She was not often around children her age, and usually had to deal with her parent's friends.

And her parents.

Not only could Isabella sense peoples' thoughts and emotions, the Sixth Sense, but she could actually sense peoples energy.

This is the Seventh Sense.

She would strike a stranger or a friend as an exceptionally intelligent child, but these were only the signs of "normal" intelligence. The things that she knew but could not yet communicate, except in brief flashes that could be observed, were the things that were truly interesting. These were usually just passed off as coincidence.

In Isabella's people didn't just have faces, smells, voices, and textures, but also mental "faces" and what in her mind would be as clear to you and I as a face, energy patterns.

For instance, she would be able to tell who was at the door. A friend would come over, they would knock, and she would without fail yell out their name. Even if it was someone unexpected, she would not miss. In her mind, she had already seen who it was. She could also tell you, if she had wanted, how many people were in a room, or a building, if she could count that high.

Furthermore, she could "feel" a person's emotions. If you tried to fake an emotion with her, and your outside did not match your "inside" a look of confusion would wash over her. She knew how you felt, how could you not?

Like all children, she didn't completely possess the concept that all people did not have this same ability. It was obvious to her that we could see, smell, taste, hear, and feel, why not the other two as well?

She had an idea though.

Of course, this was all old news to most of the Galaxy. Certainly there were groups who had not manifested or nurtured these Sixth and Seventh Senses, but there were many more who had, to the point well beyond our new, young Character's developing ability. Many species and civilizations had fairly well-advanced telepathic powers, and some operated on nothing else.

To the general observer, it just seemed like a very smart child who paid attention to conversation, and was good at guessing games, or perhaps through a lack of contact with children just seemed more adult.

Which brings us to Isabella's parents. They were a very odd pair. They married very young, and after a year decided to have a child. A year and a half after that, they divorced, very amiably. Still very good friends, they continued to raise Isabella together, with very little changes in anything beyond their relationship. They called themselves "partners in parenting" and went from there.

Her mother, Jack (short for Jacqueline) was a young woman with great, unrealized potential. She had good ideas, and talents, but hadn't gotten around to using them yet. She was a good mother, and wanted to be so. She also had lots of problems. Not necessarily of the mental order, but certainly those, too. One, she had led a strange life before she had a child, didn't have a father when she was young or when she was old, and two, had a mother who abandoned her for a stepfather and religion. In that order. Her parents were the crazy kind of parents you only read about in books and Dear Abby letters.

The sort of relationships that she was in might strike a Human as odd, again, even immoral. (Again, only by standards too ridiculous to pay any attention to.) Some Aliens, as discussed before, think Parents in general are either a bad, or at least silly, idea.

It takes a village, as they say.

Still other cultures stuck very strictly to the parenting and didn't let their children out of their sight until they were adults. (It should be noted that nowhere else in the Universe is age the marker for adulthood. It is done by mentality and ability.)

But Jack was a good mother.

Isabella also had a little sister, Ava. Ava had been born after Isabella's parents had separated, and was by a different father. She was a normal child, sweet sometimes and nasty in others. Such it is, as they say.

Isabella and Ava got along just fine, especially since Isabella could communicate with Ava in a way that no adult ever could. They took turns driving their mother crazy and very often could be found just sitting side by side, staring at a wall. This wasn't odd behavior coming from Isabella, but their mother often wondered why Ava would do it, too. Copy-catting, she supposed.

Actually, Isabella had told her that if she tried hard enough...she could see through walls.

CHAPTER 16
AND SO THE ACTION BEGINS

I am quite sure that you have been waiting for the Story to go somewhere besides every which way that you wanted it to. You want to know what the hell is up with the oatmeal, you are tired of me cutting off right when it is getting interesting. You want Characters to meet Characters, you want some explanations and you are damn sure you want the Plot to hurry up and get here.

I mean, come on, it's the 16th Chapter already!

Hey, you, it's my Story. Settle down.

And furthermore, you'll just have to wait on the oatmeal.

What you don't have to wait on is the plot.

The thing you have to realize is that most of the action that happened in the last 239 Chapters (I know it was only 15, but it sure does seem like a long time, doesn't it?) was all happening at more or less the same time. To recap, because I always wish that other Story Tellers would do just that…while I was having my first third encounter, Joe was meeting Anthony; Neil and Tony (or Tony and

Neil) were ignoring Justin, the bartender who gives strangely relevant advice at crucial moments and crashing into Dan; Josh was being Premiere of the Intergalactic police; Terry and Greg hadn't met but obviously were going to soon; and Isabella was just introduced.

Caught up? Good.

All of this was happening at more or less the same time.

And here is where things start to heat up.

Earth was going to be destroyed.

I find this out right after I have offered three Aliens some oatmeal. They had enjoyed it enough to kindly tell me that someone was going to destroy the Earth. They didn't know whom, they didn't know when, but they were sure going to try and find out.

The next thing I find out is that this was pretty standard procedure. Earth is under constant threat, simply because we are who we are. Floating around, more or less oblivious to the rest of the Universe. Most of us are more or less oblivious to any country outside of our own, but that is for another Story.

Normally, these threats are quashed politically. The real problem was whomever was planning on blowing up Earth, or whatever they were going to do, had already destroyed a couple of other large celestial bodies, just to show they were serious. They had sent out a manifesto generally stating that Earth stood for everything and anything wrong with the Galaxy. This had been a general contention on many fronts, but most Aliens just didn't care.

We just didn't make that much of a difference.

So the three Aliens that I had met and fed were there to monitor things from our side. They were all Agents of the Intergalactic Police.

Of course they were. Who else would they be?

To them, however, this was a fairly important assignment, for one particular reason.

They reported on the subject directly to Premiere Josh, whom, as you know, had a peculiar and particular interest in Earth. It was always a topic of discussion, but for thousands of years, it was a job handed down to lower officials.

We just weren't that important.

It was rumored that it had something to do with the fact that Premiere Josh liked kittens.

Really.

It might strike a person odd that the Supreme Bad-ass of the Galaxy, Premiere of the Intergalactic Police Force, and Bearer of Several Important Medals liked kittens.

Everyone has to have something, don't they?

So, my new friends were posted to watch over Earth from one of several installed outposts on Earth.

The Pyramids. Also the Steppe Pyramids. Also Angkor Wat. Also a now defunct station near the Fiji Islands. Used to be called Atlantis. (It went underwater accidentally, due to a major oversight by certain contractors.)

Now, if you are a student of geography, or perhaps just have a globe, you will be able to notice that my Pyramid in Mali and the Fiji Islands are both on the Prime Meridian, on opposite sides of the globe, almost equal distances from the equator, one above, one below. The same goes for the Steppe Pyramids and Angkor Wat.

Coincidence? I think not.

There were other Aliens stationed at the other outposts who had not been discovered, which my three (we'll call them Bob, Bill, and Biff or the Three Bees) were certain would be a matter of contention later. They had been discovered, and while this was not necessarily a punishable offense, certainly there would be some ridicule involved.

I mean, these guys were supposed to be the elite of the elite, but then again, no one was supposed to be there, either. Nor had their ship's sensors picked up any Humanoid life forms in the area. What they figured out and then told me was that the cave I had been breakfasting in must have had a mineral content that made me invisible to their sensors. As far as the door being open, that was Biff's fault.

Apparently, he was always leaving doors open.

Now, it might be interesting at this point to point out that the Aliens were definitely using some sort of technology here that was beyond what normally you would think of as observing equipment. One, there was no visible mechanics, buttons, electronics, or otherwise substantial items that could be identified as some sort of technology.

This partially explains why such well-explored areas like Angkor Wat and the Steppe Pyramids showed no signs of advanced technology, besides the blindingly obvious architectural signs.

The other part of the explanation is we really hadn't explored that well.

So, the Three Bees wandered around, or lounged about, watching projections and what can only be described as four-dimensional displays, and eating on the rest of my oatmeal, for which I had ran back to get from camp.

All things seemed normal. Occasionally, they would take (what, conference calls? Who knows.) from the other stations, through which I was found out about, and it seemed like there was much prodding and joking directed at the Three Bees, at my expense.

I think.

CHAPTER 17
PLANETARY POLICY AND CRASHES

Throughout the Galaxy, it is a general rule that you do not tell another Being about It All. If seeing you or finding you more or less brings all they "know" crashing down around them, then you can give them some background information.

It is also not kosher to lie. If asked a question, you (generally) should give the answers correctly to the best of your knowledge. Not lying falls under Rule Three of the Galactic Codified Law. Rule Four and Rule Three are the most often in conflict for individuals, but that is the nature of individual thought and perception.

Go ahead. Page 57. You know you need to.

Ok. Back? Memorized those codified laws yet?

It might come in handy sometime. You never know.

It could also be considered fairly necessary to explain yourself to a Human if you happened to be unbelievably drunk and had happened to crash your friggin' spaceship into said Human's car.

Such was Tony and Neil's predicament.

Now, as you may well know, spacecraft are made to last. Well, maybe you didn't know, because our spacecraft never seems to…however, Alien spacecraft is built to last.

Part of the reason that our spacecraft is so flimsy is because we have to make it light. In order to break the gravitational pull of the Earth, it must be light enough to propel it into space. We more or less set a ping pong ball on a stick of dynamite, and see if that won't do the trick.

Maybe it's a more complicated than that…but not much.

Since space travel is one of the measures Aliens use to gauge whether or not a planet is ready for Intergalactic Trade…we are obviously right out on that count.

Cars, however, as you may well be more or less aware, are not really built to last. There was once a car built on Earth that would've lasted for 200 years, and got 900 miles to the gallon—gallon of water, that is—and also cost $500 in raw materials, but I'll give you three guesses what happened to that.

So, needless to say, but I'll say it anyway, Neil and Tony's spaceship, while having plowed down a considerable swath of trees, and failing to miss Dan's very fast car (they were drunk, remember) was completely fine. Maybe a scratch. Maybe.

The front section of Dan's car, however, was gone. Not just broken off, but gone. Lucky for Dan, it was only the first few feet. Any more and the feet gone would be his. Also gone was the tree that he had originally hit. As were about 100 feet of trees beyond that. Just gone, in about a 15 foot swath.

Dan awoke.

Now, I am going to warn you ahead of time that Dan liked his car. Also, I will remind you that Dan did not think often about Aliens. He had other things on his mind. So Dan's initial thoughts had nothing to do with the Planetary origin of the occupants of the craft that had disintegrated the front of his very fast car.

First, the moon was out. This would have been more than enough light for Dan to see around the area, but the moon was rather unnecessary due to the HyperGlow Green in which Tony and Neil's Gravlin V3000 HyperShip had been painted.

Now, I am sure you and I both have ran into a decision not based on all the facts, or perhaps not based on any facts at all, without really thinking about or even considering how large the situation is. Furthermore, I am quite sure that you and I have both completely missed the gravity of a situation due to personal duress.

Such was Dan's situation.

Dan was angry. Expletives flowed. His door would not open, so he punched out his window and climbed out. He quickly assessed the situation, put one and three together, and still got six, even though he had skipped two altogether, and made for the green craft.

Inside the green craft, Neil and Tony were not quite sure what to do. They saw the Earth Human approaching, they saw what they had done, and due to Rule Three and their state of inebriation, they decided to go and try to explain. They got up, went to the exit, and came down the ramp.

Dan approached. Neil spoke first.

"Um…hey there. Uh…We…"

"We are really sorry," interrupted Tony.

Back to Neil.

"Yeah."

Dan looked at one, then to the other, then punched Neil right in the face. Tony's eyes widened just enough to see the second blow land between his eyes. Both fell to the ground.

Now, not having much experience in punching out drunk Aliens, I am not sure how easy it is. I can't imagine that a tap will do it. However, whatever had brought Dan to this point now left him. He looked around, his brain registered the past events, his surroundings, and skipped a beat.
Darkness.

Now, Tony and Neil, being two of the Coolest Beings in the Galaxy, very seldom get into fights. Even fewer people try to punch them, and even fewer succeed. There is always someone there to stop them. In short, neither Neil or Tony had ever been punched in the nose.

They got up, rubbing their noses.

Now, at this point, knowing full well how Humans who said they had contact with Aliens, or Alien craft, or anything at all that was "Extra Terrestrial" were treated, Tony and Neil could have just flown away, and forgotten about the whole thing.

The only problem is the one you may have forgotten.

Neil and Tony were still drunk.

Neil: "Shit that hurt!"

Tony: "Yeah. I had never really been punched in the nose before."

Neil: "Me either."

Tony: "What should we do with him?"

Neil: "Um…take him with us?"

Tony: "Yeah, that would be fun."

And thus began the first (or second or third or fourth, depending on your point of view) very bad decisions made by our dynamic duo.

CHAPTER 18
ANOTHER MEETING

Terry was more or less on the street. By more or less, I mean more, but less because it wasn't like he didn't have anywhere to go. He could get a hotel. He had money. He could call a friend. Why he decided to sleep in a corner in the subway was more-or-less one of those things that one does, simply because you have never done it before.

Most people go scuba-diving, or skydiving.

Terry was now noticing things as well. A man sitting on the opposite corner, per instance. This was a real homeless man…with no money, no place to go, no friends. The whole package, multiple layers of dirty clothing, grubby appearance, and Terry supposed, unappealing smell.

This made Terry pause, here he was sleeping on the subway in $500 worth of cloths.

He smelled fine, he was sure of it.

I guess though, one always looks good on their first day of homelessness.

As Terry drifted off to sleep, sitting on the dusty floor, the last thought that crossed his mind was what people getting on the subway in the morning would think of the interesting dichotomy that were these two corners of this particular subway platform.

Cut to: Greg Van Huesan, walking to the subway, early in the morning, talking to his assistant about getting Terry Vrais in a meeting, as soon as possible. Now, Greg knew that Terry lived nearby. He didn't know which building, he didn't know which street, but hey, they were practically neighbors.

Actually Terry lived three city blocks, exactly, from Greg.

On the same floor, in different buildings.

One of Life's little Coincidences.

Greg went down the stairs into the subway station.

Now, as an avid story reader, and perhaps a cynic yourself, you are thinking, "Right, right…and Greg sees Terry at the bottom, and BOOM! Another Coincidental meeting. How convenient."

Let me tell you why this actually happens.

Greg is not the type of person who misses much. He is also a person who notices every single homeless person he passes on the street. This is not because he is some angelic, caring soul, or anything of the sort. It is mostly because he has no choice but to notice.

It is his observant nature.

Perhaps more people notice than you would think, but most are to the point where they notice and just don't care anymore.

Or never did.

A few people had noticed that the man sleeping on the subway was dressed nicely, but hey, this was New York. You've seen It All.

Well, obviously not, but you'd think so.

And, if you have been to New York, you know very well that everyone who lives there, or has lived there, or has lived there for going on four weeks thinks that they have seen Everything.

'Tis the New York way.

Greg hadn't seen It All, it was true. And he was well aware of it. However, he had seen quite a lot, and seeing it once doesn't mean that when you see it again it has no effect. Quite the opposite.

The only Story-aiding Coincidence here is that Terry was just waking up as Greg came down the stairs.

As Greg hit the bottom of the stairs, he was saying "What do you mean, he's gone? Like disappeared-gone, or not-in-at-the-moment gone?"

Then he saw Terry's face.

He knew this face.

His phone dropped from his ear and his jaw dropped.

Now, having seen it all is nothing like having Coincidence bring your world come crashing down around you.

Perhaps this has never happened to you, but think of Life's Little Coincidences. Then think of Life's Big Coincidences.

Now think about how many of those you have completely disregarded.

Well, just imagine one that you can't disregard. A Coincidence that keeps you up for days and you never really forget about it.

Don't have one of these?

You probably just weren't paying attention.

At this point, well, at this point, now that I am done making mine, I think it is suffice to say that now Greg and Terry have met.

Coincidence? Well, if there is such a thing.

CHAPTER 19
AND A SIDE OF...

Lily found herself in the barn, to escape the hot Georgia sun that burned down like a golden sphere in the sky, bent on making her drip pearled drops of sweat. Her flaxen hair stuck to her forehead, like her tight flowered dress stuck to her round breasts and buttocks. At the other end of the barn, the farmhand, Luke, was thrusting his pitchfork into a mound of hay, hay the color of Lily's hair. His shirt lay on the ground behind him, and his rippling muscles were tan and hard, and his short brown hair and stubble were set around his startling blue eyes.

"Hello, Luke, how y'all doing today?"

"Fine, Miss Lily, and you?"

"Oh, just fine."

Lily watched with pleasure as Luke's eyes took her in, moving up her legs, pausing on her cleavage, and moving up her neck. Lily reached out and caught Luke's square jaw and pulled him close, pressing her bosom against his.

"Miss Lily…"

"Yes, Luke?"

Luke reached out and put his massive arms around Lily, pulling her close. His tight jeans already showed the fruits of her labor. Suddenly, Luke

Backspace.

Backspace.

Backspace.

Hold Backspace.

Kris Volkenstien sighed. Kris was a writer. And she was a good writer that only wrote crap. And she knew it. She knew every bit, every word, phrase, sentence was worse than the one before. Under the pen-name Veronica Renault, Kris had written 12 books— romance novels. Terrible, awful romance novels. That made more money than she knew what to do with. She was writing another because she had taken an advance from her publisher. *Never again,* she thought, *never again am I going to write such tripe.*

Her thoughts were jarred by the phone ringing.

She picked up.

"Hello?"

"Kris! Where the hell is the book? Deadlines are deadlines, kiddo, and you need to crank this shit out!"

Her editor, CJ. CJ was a bastard, but he was a great agent. Great in that he got her paid. And therefore, got himself paid, which is what he liked best. CJ liked to get paid because he liked expensive scotch and inexpensive dates (read: cheap whores).

Which brings us to a interesting point, prostitutes.

Kris was a prostitute for the soul. She wanted to write good books, and didn't. She happened to be very good at writing very bad books, and did it because there was a demand. Just like a hooker.

The people that read her books were just like johns, although, usually, janes…middle-aged women with no lives and no imaginations needing a fix.

Prostitution, as a profession, is rampant throughout the Universe. Many humans (although far less than you may think) would be appalled by this. What they don't know is that sex is not that important in the grand scheme of things, and furthermore, there are much worse things you can hand out for cash.

Much worse.

In fact, there are few better things that you could sell for large amounts of money, if you ask me.

Kris, on the other hand didn't give out sex for money in the traditional sense, but after all, she did give out sex for money.

Never again.

Well, never again after this time.

Her fingers moved back to the keyboard.

With a huge internal sigh, she thought to herself, goddess of her created world, *Oh well. Let there be crap.*

CHAPTER 20
THE PLOT THICKENS

You have probably been wondering when your eyes would be caressed again with tales of intrigue and wonder involving the Characters Joe and Anthony, whom have been paired in this particular Story out of, what was it again?

Oh yes. Coincidence.

Well, throughout all the past action, Joe and Anthony have been getting to know each other. Anthony took Joe for a ride in his spaceship, which now was not that big of a deal to Joe, as now he remembered his previous space-flight-experience. They discussed life, the past, the future, and above all else, Earth Music.

They both loved Earth Music, and since Anthony played the guitar, he was very keen on the fact that Joe did as well, and had several of them. Joe's specialty, however, was the bass guitar.

So, while Galactic political turmoil brewed, and our other Characters were busy running into each other at random, Joe and Anthony decided to jam.
And jam they did.

Loud and long. The problem was a lack of a drummer, and while both could sing, they really could have used some vocals. So what though? They were having a good time. A good, loud time.

Suddenly, Anthony stopped playing. Joe followed suit.

"What?" queries Joe.

"I just remembered I forgot something really important."

"What's that?"

"I have a drum synth on my ship."

Now, mind you, they had just taken a spin in Anthony's space rocket not two hours before. The problem is that within that last two hours, some things had changed, atmospherically speaking.

Let's not say "atmospherically"…let's say "spacially."

A red light blinks. A beeper beeps.

"Oh shit."

CHAPTER 21
THE PLOT THICKENS 2

"Oh shit."

This isn't exactly what Premiere Josh said, but it is a decent approximation. His was a little harsher, not as harsh as possible, but this was more an exclamation, an expletive of exasperation than anger.

Like if you stepped in a pile of shit.

Premiere Josh had two reports on his desk. Both of which concerned you and I, as Humans of Earth, but on far opposite sides of the Scale.

Which Scale? The one that derives the "Oh shits" from the "Yippees!"

On the one report, I can tell you now, even though I find out later, that three very large Terrelian Snippets had entered the space just beyond Earth.

A Snippet? What's in a name, really?

No, no…don't get vernacularly confused here. Snippets are big and bad. Very bad.

And Premiere Josh knew this.

Once upon a time, there was a race of Beings who, at birth, installed every person born with a tracking device, paired with a bomb. It was always placed in your lower left calf. Not lethal, per se…but not a happy situation were it to be set off. Why would it be set off? If you broke the rules. Rules like what? Rules like don't talk about your government. Rules like don't steal. Not rules like don't kill people though…this race didn't think that was such a big deal. However, if you didn't pay for parking? BOOM! Your left leg was blown off below the knee. If you happened to get your leg blown off, you were then arrested, and it was then decided whether or not losing your leg was enough punishment.

This particular practice was nearly abandoned when children of this particular race began being born with no left leg below the knee. Evolution itself was telling this race to knock it off! When it was learned that nearly every person on the planet had no left leg below the knee, that's when, Intergalactically, other Aliens started getting involved. However, unfortunately, the damage was done. Now, almost a thousand years later, every member of this bipedal race is born without a left leg, below the knee.

This race is the Terrelians. (As if you hadn't already guessed.)

Needless to say, but I'll say it anyway, this would make anyone cranky. Now, certainly, you couldn't tell that they only had one leg. Their technology had advanced to the point that they were growing and grafting new legs, attaching them, or as many of the race preferred, attaching extremely advanced bionics to that leg, then an arm, then the other leg…several of the Terrelians with more pull and more money were merely a head on a robot. They were either politicians or in the military. Go figure.

Do you know what the difference between you and a Terrelian is? Almost nothing, save that you probably don't have a propensity for being born with your left leg missing below the knee. What you will take a guess at now, and I will tell you later, is what the facts on the second report on Premiere Josh's desk.

But back to the first.

Premiere Josh had been dealing with the Terrelians forever. Since before he was Premiere. Every Galaxy has one, you know. A bad apple. A group that just isn't happy unless everyone else isn't happy. The Terrelians had been top dogs for some time, but that was thousands of years ago, and their blinding arrogance and need for universal (or Galaxial, if you will) conformity was just too much.

So they got beat down.

Now the Terrelians were just a sad bunch of mostly old men who wanted to rule again. Lately, they had been causing minor problems, and had become regarded as little more than pests by most of the Galaxy. The reports on Premiere Josh's desk, one from Aliens in the Field, Intergalactic Police Field Intelligence Division, and the other, from the Historical Society of the Galaxy, were both very alarming, and both very connected.

Josh got up from his desk, rang up to the launch bay, and headed out.

CHAPTER 22
WHAT YOU ALREADY KNOW

"Oh shit."

"What?"

"Terrellians"

"Oh shit."

At this point, while sitting in a cave, under a mountain, with three Aliens, who have told you that they are there to monitor Earth, because there have been threats towards the planet, in that it was being threatened to be destroyed, this is not the sort of conversation you would put on your "Conversations I Want to Hear" list. Not really at all.

The question had to be asked.

"Who are the Terrellians?"

And thus I was told what you already know.

The Three Bees got right to work, sending and filing a report in what seemed like a matter of seconds. Then they returned to their "routine," watching the blinking red lights, manipulating what ever it is that they manipulate, and generally going about their business.

"Don't worry,"said the "B" Biff. "We've got it covered."

Now, at this point I began wondering why a group of Aliens, who genetically speaking, were your and my brothers, would want to blow up a Planet. Why would an Alien race want to blow up another Alien race that was more or less the same Alien race? That's ridiculous!

Oh…wait.

At this point in my thought process, all Three Bees were looking at me with what can only be described as amusement. I don't know why they are so easily amused, but it is not a difficult process to amuse an Alien who is light-years ahead of you, both socially and evolutionarily.

Wait though…

Why do you care? Why does the rest of the Galaxy care? Why help us, when, more-or-less, we are just as bad as the Terrelians?

Biff answered me.

"Because, more-or-less…it's the right thing to do. Furthermore, we may have some inside information that makes Earth a very interesting place."
Inside information?

"Yes, our Historical Society may have uncovered some very pertinent info about this Planet."

Wait, the reason Earth is being saved is because it is of historical interest?

"Not really. We don't want Earth destroyed either way. And our information hasn't been confirmed yet."

Oh. I see.

Now the Three Bees seemingly satisfied with their explanation of events and Galactic Politics, went back to their work again.

It didn't seem like it was taking that much out of them.

CHAPTER 23
GODS AND CHILDREN

Isabella had found a new hobby. She liked asking questions that she already knew the answer to. At this point in her already accelerated life, these were not questions of real importance, but nor were they really "childrens" questions, if there really were such a thing. No, these were questions regarding random thoughts that she used to gauge exactly what a person was thinking. She didn't know this made her abnormal, nor did she know that it was really that big of a deal. She used these questions to put people off guard, and when their guard was down, she could see their intent.

Let's not say see, let's not say feel...let's say sense.

We can all more or less see with all of our senses. You hear a train, you can "see" it in your what, for lack of a better word or phrase, is called your "minds eye." You smell an orange, so your mind's eye sees an orange.

Isabella was normal enough, save her "mind's eye" being a little more acute than yours or mine.

You already knew this, if you had been paying attention.

Most children, when confronted with a feeling, or an experience, automatically deduce that everyone feels the same as them, knows what they know, and understands the way things work. This is true until the child hits that certain age where they know that "older people" know things that they do not. So they ask questions. Then of course comes the age when children think older people know nothing, but that is for an entire story of its own, another time.

The difference and amazing thing about Isabella was that she did know that no one else could "read" people like she could. She also knew that people guarded their thoughts, probably more closely than they guarded their wallets or their lives. This makes for a very, well, let's say... accelerated little girl.

She also found that asking a very easy, but very obscure, question was the fastest way through the proverbial gate.

Her new recent favorite circled around her new favorite food.

"What is oatmeal made of?"

Now, you and I both know right now, partly because you have oatmeal on the brain, and I already, perhaps prematurely so, gave away the fact that oatmeal plays a very important part in the story, know that oatmeal is made of rolled oats.

We're getting there.

Regardless of your knowledge of the grain cereals, this would be a question that would make you pause, were a very small child ask you, in a voice, posture and attitude quite strange for a child so small. Out of place, even.

Of course, there was Ava as well, and Ava was a good, old-fashioned child. She cried and ate and made trouble, simply because that is what babies do. Having a normal child and an absolutely abnormal child can wreak havoc on a person.

Now, to get these Characters involved in the Story.

So, Isabella, Jacqueline, and Ava were all at the grocery store. As Jacqueline looked on the shelf for some peanut butter, Isabella noticed an old man with a limp walking down the aisle. She walked to him, and started her general grilling.

"Excuse me, sir. My name is Isabella. What's your name?"

Now, first the man seemed like she had asked him what his underwear size was, but he quickly regained his composure.

"John," came the gruff reply. He continued to look around.

"John, do you know what oatmeal is made of?"

At this question came a blank stare, and with it all the room Isabella needed to step inside "John's" mind.

"O-hat-meal?"

Isabella looked him up and down. Suddenly, her sense, her sixth sense, was shut down. Not shut down so much as pushed out. Suddenly, he was a blank. She narrowed her eyes, as did he, and simultaneously, they spoke.

"You're not from around here, are you?"

Then Isabella looked down. The old man had on one normal shoe, and one metal shoe. One metal shoe on his left foot.

And as she turned to see her mother and sister picking out fruit juice, and turned back, the one-legged man was gone.

CHAPTER 24
FAME

Dan found himself on a spaceship. In space.

Now, at this point of the story, you are not shocked or even surprised by this, but that is because you have prior knowledge of the situation, both Dan's and the Galaxy's.

Let me remind you Dan had no such knowledge.

Now, perhaps with a completely normal person, the shock of this situation alone would send you into mental convulsions.

For instance, let us say for a moment that you as a person had the technological ability to, say, send a person to Arizona while they were cutting you off in traffic. ZAP! They find themselves in the middle of the desert, engine idling. Now, let us also say that also within your grasp is the technology to leave a small note saying something to the extent of, "In response to your driving like a jackass, you have been sent to Arizona. Thank you and have a nice day."

Of course, if you lived in Arizona, this wouldn't work as well.

The point is that because of the frailty of the Human mind, most people would never even get to read that note. Even if you taped it to their nose. The immediate response would be some sort of blackout, or fainting, and the secondary response would be that you would go crazy and spend the rest of your life with a irrepressible and incredible fear of driving.

This is not true of all people, as no generalizations are.

Dan was one of the types of people (although he didn't know it yet) when confronted with said situation, would get out of his car, take the note off his nose, read it, and not be affected mentally in the least, save perhaps a good dose of anger.

This is the first course of new Human evolution. Mental and emotional strength.

So, now, in a situation not at all dissimilar to being instantly transported to Arizona, and perhaps, in the reality of things, a bit more shocking, Dan did exactly opposite of what most Humans would do. He trusted his senses, rather than his sense memory. He surveyed his surroundings, he developed a theory, and came to the conclusion that he was not dreaming, nor dead, and if either of those were true, there was little he could do about it. Standing above him were two Humans (or so he thought) and they were both staring intently. Dan was succinct, as was his way.

"What the FUCK is going on here?"

His "hosts" looked from one to the other. And for probably the first time ever, missed with their cosmic ability to not step on each other's lines and started speaking at the same time. After the shock of that had worn off, Tony and Neil began a rapid (albeit not-altogether-thorough) explanation of the galaxy as they knew it. They told Dan about Earth's place and the rest of the Galaxies opinion on Earth and it's inhabitants. They told him about the law system and about the medical system, and about the very basics of Interstellar Travel. Dan listened intently, posed questions, and provided personal opinions. The surroundings no longer mattered, and good and welcome conversation was ensuing.

The first ever unofficial Alien/Human meeting was actually going quite smashingly, considering the circumstances from which it had sprung.

At the end of the conversation, Neil and Tony asked Dan if he would like a tour and a beer at the best bar they knew, and Dan would have probably agreed if he had not been rudely interrupted by a monstrous blast and subsequent shaking of the vessel in which they resided.

Tony and Neil rushed to the cockpit, and as always, right on cue, a face appeared on the large screen to the front.

In unison. "Oh shit. Terrellians."

They were locked down. A tractor beam held them in their place. The ugly face on the screen barked, "What are you doing in Earth Space? What is your business here? We will destroy you! And who are you? You look familiar. Wait a minute, aren't you..."

Here it was time to make a new point. Now, you might think, warlike, left-leg-missing, and generally just plain inhospitable beings like the Terrelians would have no idea what "cool" was and, furthermore, wouldn't give a flying Caruvian Bat shit (they're very large, ever heard the artful poem about being glad cows don't fly? You get the picture.) whether or not you had been in countless movies and had released four OHS (Optical Holographic Storage) disks of original music. But you would be wrong.

If you take the worst and most worthless people in Human Society, and I am not just talking about the people in jail, or even just the corporate bastards and the white-collar criminals. Even the worthless, pot-smoking, Bob Dylan listening, leftist activists who only really oppose what they oppose because they can't think for themselves anymore than the teeny-boppers they hate. Also take the best people in society, the truly nice people. The people who give time (the only true selfless commodity) to better society, the people who really truly care. There will be a common thread. They will get excited to meet someone famous.

They might not get all giggly, they might not pee their pants with excitement, but they will be excited.

The best of these situations is when the meeting is completely natural. In a grocery store. Or a restaurant. Or in Earth Space, on your way to destroy a planet, when you thought it was just some lowly life form waiting to be crushed.

"Tom! Kelly! Get in here! It's Tony and Neil!"

"You mean Neil and Tony?"

"THE Tony and Neil? GET OUT!"

"OH! NEIL AND TONY!"

At this point. Tony and Neil and Dan stood quite aghast, although Dan was a bit more perplexed, perhaps.

The Terrellian Captain, and his Commander (Tom, apparently) and First Lieutenant (Kelly, apparently) all caught themselves at roughly the same moment.

"Um...cough, cough...what are you doing in Earth Space? We are going to have to detain you. We are on official Terrelian business. Prepare to be boarded!"

Commander Tom leaned down and whispered in the Captain's ear.

"And do you think you have time for some autographs?"

At this point, the complete hilarity and absurdity of the entire situation hit Dan like a ton of Circus Peanuts. Sure, it's funny, but it will still knock you on your ass. He passed out due to convulsive laughter.

CHAPTER 25
TYING IT TOGETHER

Greg and Terry sat over coffee.

Coffee is a hilarious beverage. First, It is made from beans. This is uncommon, except for on Earth, where three types of beans are used to make several types of beverages. Cacao beans, for chocolate anything (hot, milk, soda, candy). Soy beans, which are the miracle bean, as they can literally be turned into anything, including but not limited to beverages. Soy beans can also be turned into other things, some edible to some not edible. Like cars. Or ink. And then there is coffee. Coffee stands out because it is the bean that is turned into, and only into, coffee. Sure, there is coffee candy, and coffee liqueur, and coffee toffee, and who-knows-what-else. But let's face it. It's all just a different form of a cup of coffee. And that is where the hilarity really begins. You would think that coffee was coffee, but of course, in all their wisdom, Humans cannot leave well enough alone. There are more variations on "The Cup of Coffee" than there are in the Human DNA chain.

Let's not get into it in depth.

Terry and Greg were having coffee. Greg, black and sweet, and Terry, cream and no sugar.

Silence had been their third companion for some time, as understanding seldom needs words to communicate itself.

Finally, Greg posed the question that really mattered.

"What do we do now?"

Terry answered his new friend, with the sweet sound of complete confusion. "I don't know."

These were both smart men. These were both men of the world. Both knew there was no way to broadcast what one knew and the other believed, in any credible medium, on any national or international platform, without being cast aside as kooks.

The problem, of course, was hard evidence. Humans are drastically different from most creatures, in that they require both Knowledge and Faith to believe anything.

Throughout the rest of the Galaxy, Faith is a concept reserved for self-application. A person can have Faith in themselves, faith in their abilities, and faith in their own mind. Everything else is run on empirical evidence.

By the numbers, as they say.

Humans were (and are) the only race left in the entire Galaxy, that run on Faith-based systems of anything. Religion, Government, Science...anything. This is not to say that Religion, Government, and Science are not practiced elsewhere in the Galaxy. Quite the contrary.

The difference between Humans and the Other Creatures of the Galaxy is that Humans are the only ones who worship a Higher Being whose existence had never been proven.

The other difference between Humans and the Other Creatures of the Galaxy is that elsewhere, good ideas were not turned into Beliefs. A good idea was just that.

A good idea.

Furthermore, religious leaders of every single other Religion in the Galaxy all had a bit different approach to perpetuation of their ideals.

They let others decide what works best for them.

If you know your History of Earth, you also know (and whether you agree or not is of no consequence) that every major war, and almost all the minor ones, were caused by Religion. The concept of God, as All-Knowing, All-Seeing, All-Terrible Being, Creator of All, was overtaken very early on by a terrible dose of Humanity. At which point, every group that had a Religion decided theirs was the best, and, they were going to fight to prove it.

Never mind that the people that started these Religions would not have wanted a damn thing to do with the Belief structures that arose from their ideas not ten minutes after they were gone.

I don't know any better than the next, but I would lay large money that you never would have caught Jesus talking shit about Mohammed, had they been about the Orb at the same time. Or vice versa, for that matter. Jesus' mistake was not teaching that loving one another was the way to go, Jesus' mistake was that he forgot to tell everyone that organizing Ideas into Beliefs, complete with buildings and effete poetry to appease the masses was a bad idea.

Had Jesus only preached Separation of Church and State along with "Love thy neighbor" and "Thou shalt not kill," the world would be a whole lot better off.

And Catholic-free, no less.

And before you get your panties in a bunch about the singling out of a single religion, let alone Catholicism, remember two things.

1. Aliens all over think every Religion on Earth is equally silly and detrimental to the growth of Humanity; and

2. Catholicism is about as much a Religion as Communism or Democracy. All organized Religions are nothing more than Political parties with all it's members making mandatory suggested party donations. Also there's a bit more corruption in Religion.

Not to mention the fact that nobody really listened to Jesus anyway.

Back to our characters.

Greg and Terry, at this point, had not much to do. They could either sit back and see what happened, but that might be longer than they had, or they could go try to tell the world, which wouldn't listen, and probably send them right to the looney bin.

They also had a third choice, one that they weren't aware of just yet. They could be abducted by Aliens, and not have to worry about these little problems, like letting the rest of the world in on the joke.

One really wouldn't call that a choice.

CHAPTER 26
ON TURNING TAIL...

When faced with Adversity, no race is more known for standing up to said Adversity than Humans. No matter how big the matter or monster, Humans will, usually, in all their wisdom, stand up and fight.

Anthony was not Human. When his ship's controls told him there were Terrelians entering Earth's solar system, he decided it was time to get the hell out.

And if you were paying attention earlier, you wouldn't blame him.

Out of all the reasons that the Aliens of the Galaxy had yet to make contact with Humans, the fact that Humans were both confrontational and well-armed was right at the top of the list.

Well-armed? Well, in a sense, yes. You see, despite being far behind the rest of the Galaxy in the sense of Technology in InterStellar travel, Medicine, Information Transfer and Storage, and various other areas, Humans had done quite well in arming themselves.

What Humans have done is create at vast offensive weapons Technology, with every ounce of defensive Technology being based on offensive.

You know what they say about the best Defense being a good Offense.

While light-years behind in other technologies, somehow Humans, in all their wisdom, had managed to figure out one of the most powerful forces in the Galaxy, and instead of using it to power their planet, they used it to blow it up.

There are very few technologies, despite what you may have seen in the movies, that can withstand a nuclear blast. You have to realize that a nuclear blast literally takes things apart at the atomic level. Disintegrating something is one thing, but to break it down not just into molecules, but into the atoms from which those molecules came, is quite a feat.

Also, very dangerous.

Aliens are well aware of nuclear technology, mainly because cold hydrogen fusion is the preferred energy source of the Universe. All this hooha you may have heard about crystal power, or harnessing the energy of the space-time-continuum, or some other nonsense, is just that. Nonsense.

If fusion is good enough to power the stars, it's good enough for you.

And certainly, Aliens use nuclear energy (both hot and cold) in weaponry, defense mechanisms, and so on and so forth, but their fear of Humans and their nuclear weapons was a simple one, described by a simple question.

Would you feel safe giving a child a knife? How about a stun-gun? How about a stick of dynamite and a book of matches?

How about giving the most childish, most technologically infantile race in the Galaxy a FREAKING THERMO-NUCLEAR BOMB?

You get the picture.

Humans hadn't even figured out how to start fusion without fission, therefore creating Nuclear waste, and the radiation that comes with it.

Now, there are several reasons this hadn't happened. One, Humans had been mired in political corruption involving oil for over a hundred years, and these hundred years happened to preclude and coincide with the discovery of fusion. Needless to say, scientists, ideas, theories, and even a couple working models disappeared over the years.

Two, Humans are, unfortunately perhaps, very quick learners. They advance quickly. Sure, they were behind, but their curiosity certainly propelled them through what had taken other races at least a 1,000 years, a mere 100.

But something that is Sentient Being Nature is to look at something for what it is, not what it has been or could be. Aliens of the Galaxy don't care what Humans are capable of, nor how quickly we had gotten to this point, but rather looked at what point we were, compared to them. This is a fault of simple self-awareness. We all judge based on self-comparison. We think a baby is not as smart as an adult, because it can't talk yet, regardless of the fact that they learn a language in about half the time we would, given similar circumstances, even though we already understand the concept of communication.

C'est la vie, non?

The point I am making here is that no Alien Race wanted to take the chance that when introducing themselves to these Humans of Earth, they would be reduced to atomic components quite quickly, if any there were any sort of communication breakdown.

Anthony wanted his atoms to stay right where they were.

What? Forget I am telling a story here?

Anthony and Joe were leaving. Now, were you smart, and I am sure you are, and were you Anthony, with Anthony's knowledge, you would probably do your best to avoid all Terrelian contact, right?

You also, I am sure, realize that sometimes even your best, well, it's just not good enough.

CHAPTER 27
CUT TO...

Up in Space, there was a bit of a quandary. The Terrelians had just boarded two ships. It now had four Aliens, three Humans, a very nasty intelligence report, and last but not least, a flight squadron of Intergalactic Police, tet a tet.

Wait, three Humans? Rewind.

Alright, you may remember that Neil and Tony are there, that accounts for two aliens. Then there is Anthony and Joe, who, if you had been paying attention earlier in the story, you would know where both Aliens as well. That's four. Then Dan, that's one Human, then Greg and Terry.

Greg and Terry?

Now, I could just tell you to trust me, they were on the ship, but that would be too easy.

Something akin to springing an impossible character on the audience at the last minute in a movie. No one appreciates that.

As you may remember, Greg and Terry were having coffee on Earth, minding their own business, and wishing they weren't.

They had walked outside the coffee shop and were just walking around. Neither saying anything, as what could be said? It seemed that there would be nothing to do but sit back and wait. Perhaps wait forever.

See, here is part of the problem with Human Nature. There is a point, when everything seems so clear, so perfectly clear, that all you want to do is sit down and do nothing about it. While at first, the Truth is exceptionally scary, after a moment, you get used to it, it settles in, and there is a certain peace about it.

Sort of like drowning.

Such was the case at this point, especially for Terry. He felt no need to pursue, or tell the world. He felt no need to do anything, really. So he sat down on a bench in a small park.

Greg, on the other hand, while certainly believing the Truth, did not know the Truth, which put him in a less peaceful mood.

Then it happened. Or rather started to happen.

Greg's Big Thing.

As Terry gazed about, and Greg paced behind him, Terry started to giggle. Greg stopped, and began to doubt. Had Terry just gone crazy? Had he been fooled by a crazy man, just because he was a fan of his writing? Greg was a man not easily duped, and his doubt was not in Terry, it was in himself.

There is no greater setback than doubting one's self, especially when believing in the integrity of one's abilities was the driving purpose and means of your life. Were you to live 20 years with very little, if any, doubt in yourself, a large wave of such said doubt would be fairly unsettling.

"What's so funny?"

"There's an Alien right over there."

Terry pointed to a middle-aged man watching the sky over the city.

Greg snapped. The wave of doubt overtook him, and he jumped on for the ride. He ran full tilt at the man watching the sky, tackling him.

Now, were you in this little park inside a big city, and you saw a man in two-thirds of a three-piece suit tackling a man at least 15 years his senior, in broad daylight, that might strike you as strange.

And even in his state of apathy, Terry's sense memory kicked in and he pursued Greg, getting to the tumbled duo just seconds after impact.

Greg was yelling.

"WHY ARE YOU HERE? WE KNOW YOU'RE AN ALIEN!"

People in the park just went about their business. This was the Big City. This sort of stuff happened all the time.

Terry reached down, grabbing Greg around the waist. The man Greg had tackled, while strangely, not overreacting, struggled to get away. Greg grabbed his ankle.

To find cold, hard steel.

The "man" opened his coat, grabbed a small device, and pressed a button.

Two seconds later, Greg's doubts were no more.

CHAPTER 28
BACK TO THE BACK

Premiere Josh was in a bit of a quandary.

He had in front of him several Terrelian Snippets, holding Human and Alien Hostages. The spiral effect of having so many huge objects in Earth's space was soon to begin.

Earth might be young, but it had plenty of eyes.

It was beginning.

Either soon Earth would know everything, and that would be problematic, or if things went extremely, impossibly well, all this trouble might be averted.

Even more troubling was the intelligence report in front of him. Thirty years of investigations had come to a head, and things were starting to make sense.

He called for his top advisor.

Now this is the point were sometimes the written word doesn't do the shock scene as well as say, a movie. So I am going to set the scene for you, so you can be delighted and surprised.

Premiere Josh is sitting in his command chair, on the battle deck. He looks concerned as he reads the holocommunicator in front of him. He ponders for a while, and then says, "Captain Je-Wel, please report to the battle deck." About 30 seconds later, to your delight and surprise, in walks...

JUSTIN! The six-armed-other-worldly bartender who gives strangely relevant advice! Of course!

Justin had actually been an advisor and spy with the Intergalactic Space Force for over 200 years. And a bartender for longer.

What better place to hide, while still gathering intelligence, than behind the bar, liquor, and words and information flowing like so much...liquor?

No place, I purport.

The report in Premiere Josh's hands was largely due to Justin's work. It was a very simple report, and it explained oh-so-much.

But first, let's go back to the Terrelian ship. The Terrelian commander now had all sort of problems, the most of which was three Humans on his ship, which was exactly two Humans more than necessary to get yourself vaporized.

The second largest problem was the problem presented in a report he was holding, not given to him but two minutes before.

The report was the first of two confirmed instances where Humans had shown signs of Advanced Mentality.

The first, a child in a grocery store, who had apparently read an aliens mind, and therefore knew without equivocation that there was extraterrestrial life.

The second, a Human that was also a "Truther," who was now in his custody.

The fact that for thousands of years, Humans had shown very little signs of Advanced Mentality was of no concern to the Terrelians. They had no moral understanding nor empathy that would make this bit of information even remotely important.

But Terrelians did understand one thing.

Being vaporized.

If they knew about Humans having Advanced Mentality, then, certainly several other Alien races did as well.

And certainly, most certainly, it made the reason that he had been sent to destroy Earth much, much more clear.

You may remember from an earlier History Lesson why the Terrelian's were so nasty. And you may also remember that those reasons happened so long ago, that (almost) none of them could remember anything beyond the insanity of their dispense of personal rights.

And now I will tell you what I had just found out, in my cave, in Mali.

Also the thing that was on the report in front of Premiere Josh.

Once upon a time, a long, long time ago, there was a Race of Aliens Named the Terrelians. During a time of great civil strife, the

Race was split down two sides. One, for Peace, Understanding, and Civil Liberties. The other, for War, Conformity, and Government Control of Everything. Instead of going to War, the former group had the excellent opportunity to leave the Planet, an option I am sure many of us have wished to possess. They found a new Planet, in a straight line from their old Planet, on the other side of the Galaxy. Thousands of inhabitants left. Pursued by the other group of warmongering kinsman, many did not get out of their solar system. But a few did. By the time they reached their new home, the few that were left landed on an uninhabited planet, which they began to colonize and inhabit and procreate upon.

And they called it Terrarth. With meant "The New" This, through lack of good documentation, and a clerical error, was changed to "The Earth."

As if you didn't know.

And to kick it all off, they renamed themselves. "Terrelian" was a name of Three Parts, each from the beginning of the Races History. "Terr", which was there generalized word for "The," "Eli" which was the specific word for "War," and the suffix "an" which meant "People." "The War People." So, when They got to their new Planet, they dropped the one thing they hated out of their name. "Eli," or "War." So now they were, "The People," or "Terrans."

Again, as if you didn't know.

This was 104,673 years ago. Today.

Everyone knows the adage that History has a tendency to repeat itself.

And it did, again and again.

After the 4th War of The New, more or less everything was destroyed. The People of Earth started all over again. The only reason this helped at all, was because of the War, they had lost all their Technology. It was back to sticks and stones and farming. Needless to say, most of them died after the war.

You may scoff at the idea, people dying because they lost their technology, but I propose that, were we to wake up tomorrow, and Earth was the way it was just 300 years ago, more than 50% of us would die.

We are quite dependant on boxed cereal, you see.

However, this was a blessing in disguise. Had they kept their Technology, they would have been found, by their old brothers and enemies.

About 2,000 years after the Terrans had defected, the Terrelian Government, in it's new power, having successfully controlling their planet, and having found new weapons technology through prosthetics research, decided that they would go find and eradicate this group that had so willfully disobeyed them.

A hundred thousand years later, they found them. Now, the reason the search had gone on for so long was that it takes a long time to scour the Universe. Second, since the Terran's had no Technology anymore, they were more or less invisible. When the Galaxy started to Unite, since the Terrelians were not having anything to do with the United Galaxy, this little Historical fact was overlooked. Earth was just an anomaly, that was all.

When Earth was found, and it was confirmed to be the Terrans, well over 2,000 years ago, it was decided by the Terrellian Powers That Be that they had better hang back, since Earth had garnered some fame throughout the Galaxy. It was a matter of discussion every year as to whether or not to destroy Earth.

Now that the Humans (called this as well now, due to another clerical error, actually due to someone's bad handwriting) were gaining Advanced Mentality, the Truth would soon be out. It was decided by the Governing Body of the Terrelians that Earth needed to be watched for signs of Advanced Mentality and set back whenever possible.

This explains lots of things.

First of all, you may have heard of the Governing Body of the Terrellians. In whispers of conspiracy theory, in the annuals of history, and so on and so forth. The name of this Governing Body is…

The Illuminati.

Illuminati, however, does not mean "The Illuminated" as the name, and Earth conspiracy theory, suggest. It means, more simply, and much less mysteriously and with a much less ominous nature, "The Blue Party" (literally "Party of Blue": "Illum" = "Party," "i" = "of," "nati" = Blue) One of several Parties in the Terrelian Government System.

There's also Green (Illumicati), Red (Illumitati), and Orange (Illumisati).

Somehow, "The Blue Party" just doesn't strike fear into anyone.

So, they did a couple of things. Like introduce Nuclear Technology. No one on Earth seemed to think it strange when the concept of Nuclear Energy went from un-thought-of theory to working model in less than five years. An equivalent would be the

Wright Brothers flying at Kitty Hawk, and then having a Concorde ready to take passengers to London a month later.

They also tried a couple of other methods before that. A really big flood once. Several diseases that just came from nowhere.

They are not, however, responsible for J.F.K., Roswell, the U.N., or TeleTubbies.

They found the Humans to be too tenacious for such insipid and low-key attacks.

It was blow up the Planet, or nothing at all.

And here was the Intergalactic Police, with their big guns and lofty ideas like, "Don't wipe out whole Planets to cover your ass."

Party poopers.

CHAPTER 29
EVERYONE GETS TO KNOW EACH OTHER

If you're a Terrelian Snippet Captain, with knowledge abounding about the reasons you are on a mission to destroy a planet, and you have the I.P.F. breathing down your neck, with their superior technology and haughty nature, not to mention the fact that you've got a holding cell full of Humans, you've got yourself an interesting situation.

This would be true if only one of the four above were true.

Four of four makes it really interesting.

The thing about men in power is that knowledge is power. The more you know, the better. Terrelian military men were absolutely notorious for being power hungry. Every leader of every party was a Commander, or General, or something or other at some point in their career. So, with this rationale, you would think that Terrelian military commanders would be knowledge hungry as well.

Not true.

The truth of the matter was, until one of them decided to try and fail, or try and succeed to take power in the government, they were more or less mindless thugs. Sent to do the informed's bidding.

Due to the fact that there can be no police force without corruption, Terrelian Snippet Captain Mike had already gained a copy of the report that Premiere Josh had read moments before, and of which you know the general points.

These things get out, you know.

So now, Captain Mike knew why he was on this mission. You would think that the knowledge would lead to a change of heart or something.

Not likely.

This particular information just gave Captain Mike bargaining chips for power. Between the report, and the knowledge it contained, and his captives, this put Captain Mike in a very lucrative and powerful position.

But back to the captives.

Deep in the bowels of the Terrelian Snippet, which is not a comfortable ship, you should know, our Characters sat around and got to know each other.

All being in similar predicaments, they thought it was a fine idea.

Anthony, being the loudest, and possibly the least polite, was the one who started the rounds. First, he was certain to recognize Tony and Neil, as they were two of the Top Ten Coolest People in the Galaxy. Joe also now knew who they were, remembering all he did and all.

The three Humans—Dan, Greg, and Terry—all just sat. Terry had a bemused look on his face, Dan a disgruntled one, and Greg, well, Greg didn't know what to think.

This was all quite a bit of a shock.

Terry, you see, having been privy to the Truth for enough time that his mind had accustomed itself, or at least numbed to the insane amount of information that he now knew. Greg, on the other hand, had just been given this information, and was still acclimating. He hadn't really thought about Aliens before.

Perhaps Aliens didn't figure much into investment banking.

Dan, on yet another hand (which is very possible, considering the non-bipedal nature of the Universe), was in a different state all-together.

He didn't care one way or the other.

Aliens, no Aliens, immense and seemingly (but not) infinite Universe, or nothing past the moon, he did not care.

What he did care about, on the yet one more hand, was that no one was doing his homework for him whilst trapped on an evil Alien spacecraft.

This paired and added, then multiplied by his least favorite of all things.

Inconvenience.

So, add to this, a nature prone to irritability, impatience, and indifference to anyone's feelings on the matter at hand, being locked up in a Alien spaceship, and you have yourself someone ready to kick some ass.

So, while the debate raged on as to which area Neil and Tony were more talented in, movies or music, Dan was thinking about what would be the best way to get back and do his homework.

Now, this may have been mentioned before, but Dan was a quite strong fellow. He worked out all the time, and this paired with his natural strength made him, well, quite strong.

Again, were you, or I, for that matter, in this same situation, we would not necessarily be thinking about punching Aliens.

Previous History on this subject, within our very own Story, should call to memory the fact that Dan is not you or I, and is quite unhindered by what we might consider common sense when it comes to punching Aliens.

You may remember when you met the Characters of our Story, that Dan discovers something important to said Story. As time went on, you may have thought it would be something of a medical vein, or perhaps at least a altruistic one.

What Dan actually discovered is two fold.

One, fiber is very, very good for you, and two, Terrellians are big, big weenies.

CHAPTER 30
THE TRUTH ABOUT OATMEAL

By this point in the story, you are probably getting very tired of two things.

A) The action switching all about. Right when you think you are going to find out something, you are jerked about, and sent to another part of the story.

I have to keep you interested somehow, don't I?

B) That there has not been a damn thing about oatmeal for a long time, and furthermore, what is the deal with the freakin' OATMEAL?!

Fear no more, my friends, your questions are about to be answered. From now on, more or less, the Story will follow a more traditional story-type-pattern…and if you didn't mind the jumping all about, well, hopefully you won't mind this either.

If you had been hating the book up until this point, sorry, but why are you still reading?

If you don't like the taste, what's the point?

Oatmeal, as you may very well know, is full of fiber. Now, we as Humans know that fiber is good for you. It helps the body digest and rid itself of waste. It comes in many forms, and is in lots of things we eat, however, little on Earth carries the fiber impact goodness of oatmeal. This has already been explained. Moving on.

Something that you didn't know, however, are the mechanics of Terrellian weapons. You also probably have no clue whatsoever as to the gastronomic culture of these same Terrelians.

Long ago, the Terrelians had an excellent culture du cuisine. They ate very well, healthy, and for the most part, balanced diets.

This was very, very long ago.

When the Terrelians first started fighting amongst themselves, thousands and thousands of years ago, the first thing to go was the food. Between rationing and destroying their planet, things got less and less tasty, and more and more nutritionally defunct.

Just one more reason as to why these fellows were so grouchy.

As time went on, the entire planet was eating more or less pills and tasteless bars, filled with only the essentials. Occasionally, they would eat meat, but roughage and fibrous meals they had not.

This, as you may well know, can lead to constipation.

Just one more reason as to why these fellows were so grouchy.
So, after all this time, the Terrelians, even though they were living, on average, much longer than Humans, they more or less consisted on meals of protein, vitamins, and fat.

This had been going on for some time.

Now, for all their nastiness, the Terrelians really didn't cause that much trouble. Certainly, they were known throughout the Galaxy as being very nasty, but this was just as much disposition as anything else.

They also, like pretty much every other race, had weapons of mass destruction at their disposal. This makes you nasty, no matter what your disposition.

The truth behind the matter was, no matter how much they could blow up, they couldn't do much in the means of hand to hand combat.

Due to infighting over the years, the Terrelians had developed their weapons to fight Terrelians. At what point it was decided that these weapons would have the effect they did, and/or by whom this was decided was too far in the past to really remember.

The effect, however, was the same on every race of Aliens they had encountered and therefore seemed to be the perfect weapon. They had even tested on Humans before, and since the effect seemed just as, well, effective, an alternative was never pursued.

The effect of this nonlethal, yet very painful and effective weapon?

It solidified your bowels.

It solidified your bowels, sending you into contortions and pain unlike any you would dare to think of. Uncomplicated would be an understatement. The weapons name?

The "Shat Gat."

You may already see where this is going.

First, I know that it seems both peculiar and convenient, that the name of this Terrelian weapons Technology is named with two words you recognize as Earth Slang.

You may have forgotten that the Universe is seldom run on convenience and coincidence.

In our Universe, there is very little convenience, and even less coincidence.

First, it must be pointed out that the Terrelian's nastiness was not confined to disposition. It spread into their culture, their language, and even their hygiene.

Terrelians swore a lot. They seldom spoke a word of kindness, if ever, and were just as likely to call each other nasty names as they would be you or me.

Therefore, this explains half the name of their gun, starting with "Shat," which is past-tense for the colloquial verb "shit," which also acts as noun, adjective, and, on occasion, adverb.

The truth of the matter is, that "shit" is not a English, Human, or Terrelian word. It is older anyone can imagine, and has more variations than you can count. That it has found it's way through hundreds of thousands of years, untainted, if you could say such a thing about "shit," is quite a feat.

It helps that feces is also the substance affected by said gun.

Second, the word "Gat." Now, you may, if you are a avid listener of rap music, recognize this term. You may also recognize this term if you have ever watched a movie with a "street gang" in it, or if you have ever known anyone who is stupid and refers to guns as "gats."

You may also think that this particular phrase comes from a shortening of name of a particular weapon of mass destruction, the gatling gun.

This is only half true. The Gatling Gun, "invented" and patented by Richard Jordan Gatling in 1862, was actually a Terrelian invention. Gatling was an inventor who claimed to be a pacifist and had invented farm equipment all his life. Suddenly, right before the dawn of the Civil War, an American (Americans were not known for their weapons engineering skills) invents a new weapon of mass destruction in a matter of weeks?

Not likely.

The "Gatling" gun was given to ol' RJ in 1862 by the Illuminati.

That his name happens to contain the Terrelian spelling of the the word "gun"?

Now, that, my friends, is coincidence.

A coincidence that the Terrelian Illuminati had no choice but to view as hilarious irony. No one accused the Terrelians of having no sick sense of humor.

Then it happened. Two guards came to check on the prisoners. They turned off the force field on the cell and stepped into the room. The jovial (for a jail cell) mood turned silent. Everyone quickly found a bench and sat.

Everyone except Dan.

"SIT DOWN, YOU SCUM!" cried one of the guards.

"Yeah, we wouldn't want to have to zap your stupid ass, you vomitus wretch," said the other guard.

Everyone looked to Dan.

Dan stood firm.

"Did you not hear me, you vile pile of bile?" said Guard Number 1.

"Sit DOWN, you hulking mound of Caruvian Bat shit!" yelled Guard Number 2, brandishing his gun.

Dan did not comply. Instead, he sprang forward, punching Guard Number 2 right in the nose. He crumpled, like a piece of tissue paper in the hands of a child on Christmas, and as he fell, Guard Number 1 got off a shot. The green ray hit Dan squarely in the stomach, doubling him over.

Guard Number 1 laughed, and the four non-Terrelian Aliens in the room groaned the groan of pity reserved for when someone gets kicked in the balls. (This, by the way, hurts everywhere in the Universe.)

The curious part of the situation, beyond what happened next, was that Guard Number 2 was on the ground, holding his face, sobbing. Back to that in a minute.

Dan straightened out.

To him, it felt like he had been hit with a wad of paper in the stomach. His reaction had been purely visual. A green ray had been shot at him, he had expected great pain and overreacted.

Now, while the psychology of this is easy to explain, the physiology is even easier.

Dan was just too full of oatmeal, and therefore fiber, for the Shat Gat to do a damn thing to him.

Dan looked at the sobbing Guard Number 2, then to the confused and horrified Guard Number 1, and then a very satisfied and perhaps evil-looking grin spread over his face.

Oatmeal had just saved the day.

CHAPTER 31
FEAR AND LEADING

Captain George the Terrelian heard about the disturbance in the brig just slightly too late. As he ran to the lift to take him to deck 18, a Human, grinning, his cloths torn, punched him right in the nose.

The ship was in disarray. Those without bloody noses had even worse fates, their insides solidified by the several shat gats taken by the prisoners.

Now, this brings us to an interesting point.

Humans, by most standards, are easily scared. This can be explained through simple analogy. If you are constantly walking in the rain, isn't it likely you will get wet? Humans, unlike most Aliens, live in a constant state of fear. In fact, in most countries, a constant line of thought is:

"If you're not afraid, you're not a patriot."

They are either afraid of the unknown, or afraid of the known, or afraid of not knowing what should be know, ad infinitum.

Most Humans, if placed in a situation in which their fears are realized, will react in a manner exactly opposing to their nature. Fear either turns to adrenaline, or it turns to anger, which turns to adrenaline. This adrenaline turns into "courage," or "stupidity," to pitch a tent in both camps.

Aliens, on the other hand, are not often afraid. It is not that they are never afraid, nor that they are never angry, nor that they are never stupid.

The numbers are just lower, that's all.

So, since Anthony, Joe, Neil, and Tony were not really afraid at all, they did not pick up weapons and fight their way to the bridge. Neither, for that matter, did Terry.

Greg did. This was not necessarily because Greg was afraid or angry. It was more that it seemed like a good idea. If you will remember several pages back in our story, Greg had also had a bowl of oatmeal for breakfast every morning. He was also impervious to the shat gat. Since none of the others made any sort of connection, nor could have they, for that matter, they just assumed that Humans were impervious to the weapons, for some unknown reason, suffice to say that reasons dietary were not on their short list.

As they all came onto the bridge, and had detained Captain Mike, the discussion ensued as to what was the logical next step.

They didn't need to make a decision.

Premiere Josh's face leapt to the viewscreen.
"Terrelian Captain! This is the Premiere of the I.G.P.F.! Power down your weapons and…what the hell?"

The group stood, and since there was no appointed leader, just an appointed nose-puncher, they looked from person to person to see who would take charge and speak up.

Of all people, it was Joe.

Now, I realize that Joe has taken something akin to a back-seat in this Story, but you need to remember that Joe is new to all of this. He was not, however, new to being a Leader.

If you remember back a little further in the Story, Joe was a revolutionary on his planet.

The Truth of the matter was, Joe was a Born Leader.

See, Leaders are born, not made. This is an age-old concept dating back to well before Humans, and really well before anyone could remember.

This is not to be confused with Leaders who are born into being leaders. There are several very bad leaders in History who really where just given the post because their pappy had it, too. This is almost always a patriarchal methodology, and furthermore, almost always ends in disaster.

See, the real point in the matter is that Leaders, regardless of which side they lead, or whether they stand for "Good" or "Evil," they always have one thing in common: The ability to make people think that whatever said Leader is saying was their idea in the first place.

This is also, more commonly, known as "manipulation."

All leaders are manipulators. The good leaders, the great leaders, the bad leaders, the horrible leaders. They all have that one thing in common. Without this little trick, simple Sentient-Being, nature would invoke nothing but chaos, as everyone would want to do their own thing.

Good leaders, regardless of their end, make sure everyone thinks they are doing exactly as they like, when in actuality, they are doing what is best (or worst) for the group.

And the real trick is making it look easy.

The other truth about Born Leaders is that they seldom are given the job. They just take it, but only because no one else will.

Such was Joe's case.

Joe was a Born Leader, but frankly, anyone in the group could have taken this particular position, in this particular situation. They just all happened to wait longer than he did.

Someone, much smarter than I, once said...

"Apathy is the quickest road to obscurity."

Let's break something else down here.

You have to understand, being a Born Leader, unfortunately, puts you in a situation of responsibility.

However, everyone who is not a leader is not necessarily a follower.

Let's take our little group of cosmic comrades. Oddly, though perhaps not, there was not a follower in the bunch. Only two were Born Leaders though.

Joe and Greg.

Neil and Tony could be leaders if the situation warranted, but they could seldom be bothered with such nonsense. It's not that they were lazy (though sometimes they were) and it's not that they were irresponsible (though History seems to often speak otherwise) and it's not that they didn't care. It's just the Tony and Neil were a true Team. One was no more important than the other, especially to each other. Important and Urgent decisions could not be made, if for no other reason than each was always willing to give the other top-billing.

As a leader, indecision is right out.

As is politeness, on many occasions.

Anthony, Dan, and Terry were all a totally different kind of Leader. They were all Self-Leaders.

This is not necessarily a position of selfishness, nor apathy, nor unconsciousness, but could be a combination of any of these traits.

A Self-Leader does not necessarily care about what others do, as long as it does not affect them, or their path. Furthermore, they feel each Being (including themselves) is responsible for their own path and their own actions. Even further, a Self-Leader protects himself or herself against anything threatening him/her or the things he/she cares about.

There are, like so many things, many categories of Self-Leader, and Anthony, Dan, and Terry were all excellent versions of four of those categories.

Anthony was an Irresponsible Self-Leader. His own path is often followed by others, but he assumes that is their choice and they are big boys and girls that do as they please, and it is not his responsibility to act differently. In fact, it is his dire responsibility to be himself. It is certainly not his responsibility to tell others what to do.

Dan was a Manipulative Self-Leader. He had his way, and he didn't care what your way was, as long as it didn't affect his way. He assumed (correctly) that you were probably not going to use, choose, or lose his way, as his way was extremely difficult. He had no problem using inherent Leading skills to get his way, go on his way, or about his way. He could meld and mold, tell and be told, but he was always aware of his situation and position, which made him dangerous at times.

Terry used to be an Unconscious Self-Leader. That simply means he went about his way without really thinking about it. If he manipulated to get his way, it was usually in small doses, and he didn't really know he was doing it. He accidentally led and molded people through action and word, but didn't recognize that as Leading. Now, however, Terry was an Observing Self-Leader. He watched, he listened, and because he knew the Truth, was seldom concerned with anything not related to the truth. Observing Self-Leaders never say more than they have too.

Joe, though, was a Born Leader. As was Greg. Greg was still a little disposed as of late (you would be, too) and was probably a bit slow on the draw.

So it was Joe, who accidentally, and not all-willingly, took the role of Leader and explained to Premiere Josh the situation in whole.

The situation now was this. There were still two more Snippets, which meant two more problems. Premiere Josh's first instinct was to whomp the ever loving piss out of them, but that wasn't necessarily the right choice, giving a full scale space battle right over

Earth would be bound to draw some attention. Also, with all the information he had now, perhaps simple situation manipulation ("diplomacy" in English) was the best route.

Or maybe he could just send the nose puncher.

No, no. Subversion is always best.

He asked to speak to Terrelian Captain Mike.

After a short discussion, involving both promise of reward, and threat of violence (a ancient strategy) Premiere Josh convinced Captain Mike that they all, considering the situation, needed to get the hell out of this solar system. He pointed out it would also behoove him to send the other ships home, considering, and what reasoning he gave to get that done was of no concern to him.

Captain Mike complied. He told the other two Terrelian Captains there was an upheaval at home, and several high-ranking, high-paying positions were open, and they went, sans haste.

Such is the promise of power. It often leads to blind decision making.

Premeire Josh took in to custody the remaining Snippet, her crew, her guests, and...

...her information.

Earth was safe.

Well, from Aliens, on that particular day. From ourselves? We are not that lucky.

CHAPTER 32
HOW I KNOW WHAT I KNOW

Right now, in the time line that is this Story, I know very little of this Story. How I come to find out this Story isn't much of a story.

The moment you just read about had happened about 30 seconds before the moment you are about to read about.

Back on Earth, you may remember, I was with three Aliens. Before all of the previous "went down," I had learned a bit about my hosts. Where they were from (Deneb el Delphinus. Epsilon Delphini) and what their interest in Earth was.

Some of them had relocated here. About 20,000 years ago. And had been living on Earth, with us and among us. Why? Because we had lots of salt water that no one was using.

If you know Latin, you know who.

The Dolphins.

In their other form, they only slightly resemble Humans, and only slightly resemble dolphins, but with much more glowing.

You most certainly have heard of the theories and sailors tales of Mermaids and Mermen, then you most certainly have heard that it was really just Dolphins or manatees (who, incidentally, it never was, nor are, manatees Aliens) and certainly have heard that Dolphins really ARE Beings/Aliens/People of some sort and that they can change shape and so on and so forth.

It's all true.

So, their interest in keeping Earth safe is obvious.

Oh yeah. Atlantis? The Dolphins.

Why there are Pyramids and pyramidic objects on several continents?

Dolphins.

Moving on.

So, I had learned all of this, and apparently, the Three Bees had been privy to most of what was going on up above Earth, and I was not.

I understood what happened next though.

Suddenly, Premiere Josh came up on the screen. He quickly explained the situation to the Three Bees, and they all congratulated each other. Perhaps on a job well done, although I hadn't really seen them do anything.

Premiere Josh also explained a new situation. Due to the fact that he had captured the lead Snippet, he had found an interesting report about a Terrelian running into a small Earth Child that had Mental Abilities. The child now really truly knew about Aliens. Also, about another Human on board who knew the Truth, and who's head hadn't exploded yet. Also about how apparently, Humans were immune to Shat Gats.

Then the Three Bees introduced me to Premiere Josh. I seemed to pose a whole other problem.

"Just what we need. One MORE Human on board."

A pause.

"Bring him up."

And so, my friends and readers, this is when I, for the first time, traveled into space. It is also when I met the other Characters in the Story, and we all became smashing friends.

I actually knew who Terry was, having read some of his work, and you can imagine my surprise to see Dan, of all people, because I had known him since I was ten.

Small world, huh?

Now, at this point, you can be sure that we are talking loads of Coincidence.

Haven't you learned anything?

The Truth of the matter is, that this sort of thing only happens to certain types of people. All the Beings in this story are a certain type of Being. Random occurrences are when you bend over to tie your shoe, and find a shoelace. That's Coincidence. Running into a good friend in a spaceship just has to be something else.

The problem most people have with giving up on Coincidence is that usually, it also means you have to start believing in Fate, that things happen for a reason.

The thing is, things DO happen for a reason.

The difference between "happening for a reason" and "Fate" is that Fate as a concept means "predestined." This is the one thing that nothing is. Predestined.

Fate and Destiny run hand in hand, Fate being all things bad and Destiny being all things good.

Actually, they are both crocks.

Nothing is predestined, but everything happens for a reason.

PARADOX! DUALITY! Both true.

Let's try to explain very simply by using the simplest of all explanative methods, Quantum Mechanics.

I will not for one more second pretend that I really understand a damn thing about Quantum Mechanics, but I will tell you the basic principle.

Every second creates a new future. Your future is constantly changing. Imagine a walking through a door, and having 50 bajillion door to choose from next, step, and repeat.

Such is life.

So, everything happens for a reason. What that reason is might be as simple as what you had for breakfast (ahem), or as complicated as a chain of events completely out of your control, beginning 104,673 years ago.

So, everything happens for a reason, but nothing is decided before it happens.

So simple it's confusing, I know.

The problem people have is that they think that if something "happens for a reason" then it is destiny, and that was supposed to happen no matter what. What they don't realize is that if they had done something, anything, different on one day, nothing would be as it was at that moment. When and where is of no concern. But I can give examples.

If Dan hadn't gone to the store.

If Terry hadn't drank in the bathtub.

If Anthony had paid attention to his landing spot.

If I hadn't gotten up early.

If Greg hadn't read the paper.

If Jacqueline hadn't gone to the store.

If Joe hadn't bought an island.

The list goes on and on.

Next time something crazy happens to you, you run into a friend on the street that you haven't seen for five years, remember that if you add up, or subtract mere seconds during the hour before that, you would have missed your friend. Just let it boggle your mind for a bit, then move on.

There is very little coincidence.

Then again, some things are just unavoidable.

CHAPTER 33
A BAD DAY AT THE PARK

If Jacqueline hadn't gone to the store, Isabella would have never met an Alien, and they never would have been abducted in broad daylight in the middle of a park by a bunch of Aliens.

Some things are just unavoidable.

Jack had taken her two daughters to the park, and without warning, they were on a spaceship.

Now, you might be wondering exactly how any given Alien might find a single, solitary child, even if they happened to have a very general idea of the geographic location of said child.

I don't know. Use your imagination.

Just listen to the Story.

Jack had decided to go to the park because sometimes Isabella would start running in circles, and would not stop, unless you went somewhere. This was not because she was a special child, or even because she was abnormal, this was merely because sometimes, she could be a huge pain in the ass.

When they got to the park, Isabella went about her friendly ways, meeting people, talking to inanimate object, etcetera…when suddenly, she was face to face with a man in an overcoat.

Jack had her eye on Isabella, of course, and as we all know, strange men in overcoats in the middle of the day in the park is not usually a good thing.

It wasn't necessarily a good thing in this instance, depending on how you look at things, but on the whole, with the whole saving of the Planet thing, it's probably best it happened this way.

As Jack called for and came for Isabella, she had a very short conversation with the man in the overcoat.

"Excuse me, sir? Why do you have six arms?"

And so I met the last of the Characters.

They were brought on board the same ship as the rest of us, all of us soon to be headed to a far off planet, for reasons we, and you were/ are soon to find out.

The reason, dear friends, behind this entire gathering/kidnapping, was that the Universal Community Committee had called a Tribunal, to decide whether or not Earth should be now be let in on the joke.

The report that Premiere Josh had acquired raised interest in whether or not Humans Mental Abilities had advanced to a point where Humans could handle any or all such nonsense as finding out about half of what they know to be true just plain isn't.

Now, again, it is my personal experience that Humans hate being wrong. I myself hate being wrong. We see all too often someone pointedly shown that what they thought to be true, simply was not, and they still don't care.

This rationalization, that whatever it was that you were literally basing your entire existence, or purpose, or purpose for action upon is no longer important, simply because your idealogue was crumbled before your eyes is one of Humanities greatest powers and greatest weaknesses.

When you have to see that the world just isn't flat.

The rest of the Galaxy is less concerned with the application of mental abilities than it is with the existence of said mental abilities.

Which brings us back to Isabella. Not only was the no longer dormant telepathic trait present, This little girl had shown incredible stocism in finding and using the powers that everyone possesses, but know Human knows how use.

Even Aliens are impressed by composure in youth.

Interestingly enough, however, was that Isabella's mother just really didn't seem that surprised. Isabella had, after all, been talking about Aliens for the past few days, and she always did have something strange about her when it came to such things.

And maybe having kids prepares you for anything.

CHAPTER 34
TRIBUNAL

No matter what, no matter what culture you find, far and wide, high and low, Alien or Human, you will find the Sage Effect.

The Sage Effect is what a person who is considered very wise has on the people who consider said person wise. In the Universal Community, there were three people considered so wise that they were given the positions of Judicators on the Tribunal Court of the Galaxy.

It was, of course, these three that came up with the Universal Codified Law of the Galaxy.

Sam, Chris, and Bryan. Simple names, yes, but that is what they are called.

They were all so old, no one could remember how old they actually were.

Including them.

Not knowing how old you are does not make you unwise. If fact, probably the opposite of that is true.

A Tribunal had been called by the Judicators, because of this wacky Earth mess. What to do, what to do?

A Tribunal of this sort had not happened for a long time. So long, in fact, the Judicators couldn't even remember when. They had to look it up!

Having to look things up does not make one unwise.

Last time they did this, apparently they called a bunch of people from the Planet who had proven themselves worthy, and each of them gave reasons as to why or why not that particular planet should be considered for membership.

The Judicators—Sam, Chris, and Bryan—decided since there seemed less time for this now, the Humans who knew about the situation would have to do, and the Aliens involved would work for outside opinions too. A sampling of Beings, rather than a selection of Beings is just as good as any, they supposed.

And so a Tribunal began.

We were all invited to the Center of the Galaxy, High Universal Court.

The Center of the Galaxy was the logical spot, as it was easy for everyone to find.

Perhaps if you were me, or someone else, or even maybe yourself, you would have expected the High Universal Court to be pretty impressive.
Not really.

There were more Beings gathered outside than I could count, but the actual Court itself was some park benches and folding chairs in a very nice park. I asked about it, and was told, "Who needs pillars and dark wood to make good decisions?"

Makes sense, I guess.

The Judicators were dressed casually, although, perhaps I am not the best just of that, not really knowing exactly what they were wearing, except Judicator Chris, who was wearing something very recognizable.

Nothing.

Who needs cloths to make good decisions?

And so, really, the Tribunal began quite uneventfully, save the naked Judicator. Each of us was asked to come and make a case for or against Earth, and then decide what we ourselves wanted to do. Earth stays the same, a protected planet, left to it's own path, or introduced to the rest of the Galaxy. Go back to Earth or roam the Cosmos as one of the Community. (This part was for the Humans, obviously the other Aliens were already in the Community.) We were told there were no rules or regulations, that if we went back we could do as we wished, regardless of whether or not Earth was brought into the Universal Community. We each got one vote, as did the Judicators. Majority rule.

The Judicators warned us that the event was being televised to the Entire Galaxy, but not to worry, most Beings would be watching something else.

There were lots of other Beings there, in the park/court. The craziest thing about it was they all kept totally quiet.

The Judicators huddled together for about ten minutes and then spoke.

Judicator Sam: "We have decided."

Judicator Chris: "The Tribunal will be conducted Alphabetically."

Judicator Bryan: "The Judicators have spoken."

They sat.

So, by Judicator ruling and wisdom, Anthony went first.

Anthony was more or less for the introduction of Earth to the Galaxy, and vice versa. He said he liked the Humans he met, and that he liked oatmeal and Earth music. In the end though, he didn't really care. One vote for yes. In the end, Anthony was the type of guy who would just as soon involve everyone. The more the merrier, as they say. Furthermore, he just really didn't care.

Ava was next. (You may have forgotten Isabella had a sister, and she was definitely along for the ride, as was her mother.) The Judicators all agreed that it didn't matter what she had to say, or if she could say it, but she deserved a vote. As for reading thoughts telepathically, which would have been a good idea save that it was slightly rude, it's not very easy to read the thoughts of children. They don't know why they are doing what they are doing half the time. Ava sat on the chair and looked around. She got off the chair and crawled over to the Judicators and sat down on the grass in front of them. Judicator Bryan asked her if she thought Earth should be let in to the Universal Community. She looked at him, raised her eyebrow, and then, to everyone's surprise, especially her mother's, she shook her head back and forth, and said "Na na na," which everyone knows is baby talk for no. One vote for no. As for out in the Galaxy, or back to

Earth, the Judicators agreed that she should stay with her mother until she changed her mind.

When Dan got to the stand, his first statement was that he didn't really care and that he would really rather be studying, but what the hell, since he was here anyway. He actually thought about it for a minute, and then said that he didn't think it was a good idea. Humans couldn't handle it, as most of them were not that smart in the first place. Furthermore, quite a few of the Aliens he had met pissed him off. He didn't care about that either. He just wanted to eat some oatmeal and get back to becoming a doctor. Two votes for no. As for staying or going, he was staying. Too much work to do.

Greg was still in a state of mild shock when he sat down with the Judicators. He had been pondering over the subject and his reaction to finding out about the Universe, and he really seriously weighed the problem. Could Humans handle it? Even if they couldn't at first and there was chaos, would that be worth it? Greg's good heart won him over. He decided that despite their problems, Humans were ok. The Human spirit could get them through it. Two votes for yes. As for staying or going, oh, he was going. There was too much to see.

Isabella walked up to the bench next, without anyone telling her to do so. She knew that "I" came after "G" and she hadn't met anyone there had a name starting with "H." She sat down, and Tribunal Judicator Sam asked her if she thought it was a good idea if Aliens came to Earth, and Humans went wherever they wanted to go and that everyone knew about everyone, and so on and so forth. Isabella sat for a minute, her chin cupped in her hand. She looked around, she felt around. She looked to her mom, and she made her own decision, as she was so prone to do.

"No. I think it's a bad idea. People aren't ready." Three votes for no. She started to get down, and the Judicators asked her if she wanted to go back to Earth, or stay and explore the Galaxy. Earth now, she said...Galaxy later.

Jacqueline came to the bench, bewildered. This was all a little overwhelming, she said. And while she didn't really think about it all that often, until now she realized that her daughter, who was three, was so often right about things it was frightening. This still same child that ate crayons and didn't quite understand why it was naughty to chop up her clothes with the kitchen scissors. Humans, including but not limited to her, were not ready for Aliens. Four votes for no. Oh, and please, please back to Earth.

Joe, being an Alien after all, and Aliens are naturally more proactive than Humans, and a Born Leader, which are naturally more proactive than really anyone else, decided that the only way for this to work was the best way, which in his opinion, knowing what he now knew, was to spring it on them. No chance to react. Revolution. And start in New York, were people will be less likely to think it really that strange. Three votes for yes. Joe had also been informed that on his home planet, he had been elevated to some sort of folk hero, and it was now the loudest planet in the sector.

Premiere Josh (it was decided the Title didn't count for Alphabetical Order, this took the Judicators 12 minutes to decide, which is neither long nor short when you think about the subject) was completely for the integration of Earth. First, really, they were just old Aliens that had forgotten they were Aliens, and now was as good a time as any. And he understood that there was lots of nasty crime on Earth, and he was all about cracking down on that as soon as possible. Also, he understood that there were lots and lots of needy kittens there. Four votes for yes.

Justin thought it would be a great idea to integrate Earth. One, he was really ready to give up Spying, and maybe he could open an

Atomic Cat 2 somewhere cool on the Planet. He had heard those Humans sure can drink. Five votes for yes.

Then it was my turn. You may have forgotten, because I am not in the story that much, but my name is Os. My take? Let the Humans have it. I would cruise the Galaxy, and what happened over there was really none of my business. But at least tell them, you know…drop some pamphlets or something. I was off to see the Galaxy. Six votes for yes.

Neil technically would have been next, but first the Judicators had to decide if Neil and Tony were a team and should get two votes, but go at the same time, or if it was actually Tony and Neil, and maybe Terry should go next, or if they should have to go separately, and each get the one vote, but Judicator Sam was sure it was Tony and Neil, and Judicator Bryan was sure it was Neil and Tony, and Judicator Chris was sure he loved their last movie. It was finally decided that Neil and Tony, or Tony and Neil (depending on personal preference) were individuals, no matter how good of a team they were, and that they each got one vote and had to go in Alphabetical Order.

Neil was all for it. After all he said, maybe there are some really cool people on Earth. He even thought the guy who punched him in the nose was pretty cool. And frankly, he didn't understand why it had taken so long in the first place. He thought for sure there had been enough signs that they weren't alone in It All. Seven votes for yes.

Terry, who knew the Truth, didn't have to say much. He voted no. Humans are not ready. The chaos and turmoil following would almost certainly be more trouble than it was worth.

Five votes for no.

Tony agreed with Neil, not because he had to, or was expected to, but just because he figured Humans would be ok in the end, and hey, if nothing else, it was a new place for a concert.

Eight votes for yes.

The Tribunal Judicators of the Universal High Court then decided it was time for lunch, and that they would make their votes afterwards.

They started to take off without really saying anything else. I wondered out loud when we would reconvene. The answer seemed simple enough.

"Um…after lunch," said Judicator Chris, and then I heard him say something under his breath about how Humans might be alright, but they need to learn to listen.

So we went to lunch.

After a long lunch, we went back to the High Tribunal court and waited about 15 minutes for the Judicators. When they finally arrived, Judicator Bryan apologized for their tardiness.

"Sorry," he said. "Our service was just terrible. We waited 15 minutes just to get a drink!"

"Yeah, and then you had to make a big deal and get your salad comped, which took up time, too, you bitching at the manager," piped in Judicator Sam.

And so the Tribunal restarted.

Judicator Chris: "Ok, what's the count again?"

Judicator Sam: "Eight yes, five no."

Judicator Bryan: "Oh geez, this is going to suck."

The looks of confusion at both vernacular and statement must have abounded, because Judicator Bryan quickly clarified.

"We all voted no."

Cried Judicators Sam and Chris, simultaneously.

"Freakin' ties!"

CHAPTER 35
EASY PEASY

Now I don't need to tell you that no one likes a tie. The Truth of the matter is, people hate ties because they rob you of either the glory of success or the pity of defeat. In their ambiguity alone, it is annoying at best.

This is not a Human trait. Aliens hate ties, too, maybe even more so.

Nobody, in the whole Universe, likes a tie. This is not because of some cosmic need for winners and losers. It is simple because people like clear outcomes, and they all so hate wasting time.

Normally, the situation in the last chapter would have been easily avoided by either leaving Ava's vote out, since she was only eight months old, or adding another person to the panel. Hell, they could have used Captain Mike, for all you may care.

But, you know, hindsight is 20/20.

You may wonder how three of the wisest people in the Galaxy happened to overlook the possibility of such an occasion. Being wise doesn't necessarily mean you are efficient.

But you see, instead of doing it like Humans, who would have sent the subject to a new committee after months of posturing for spots on said committee, then they would have buried the subject in bureaucracy, and then had to start all over again, with new committee selections, and so on and so forth.

Aliens, and especially wise ones, take the easy road first.

"Anyone want to change their vote?"

The Judicators asked first if anyone wanted to change their vote, and when no one spoke up, asked if anyone would like give a little sway speech, and go from there.

They didn't have to do that.

It was Terry that decided to change his vote. He stood up and made it known that he was changing his vote. And then he explained why. The Truth, and he knew it, was Humans would not react well to finding out that they were tiny little insignificant Beings in a Galaxy full of other Beings, and even more so, they would be pissed to find out that Tolerance and Equality were key drivers in the Galaxy as a whole. They would be mad because now they had even MORE people they needed to learn how to like. The Ignorance that breeds Racism seem even sillier when you increase the reasoning behind it from just the color of your skin, or the name of your god to how many arms and legs or eyes and mouths you have.

The Truth was Humans wouldn't take it well.

But the other Truth was, they needed to take it, one way or another.

You see, sometimes, the good for all doesn't seem good at first. Dollars to doughnuts that if Humans, and any Humans, met another race, that was exactly like them in EVERY way…red, yellow, white, black, brown, or purple with pink polka dots; Christian, Muslim, Taoist, Buddhist, Atheist or Jewish; and any combination of the two, but that other race just happened to have three eyes? Oh yeah, hatred would abound.

Not because we're stupid. Because we're silly and very, very nearsighted.

And because we're stupid.

Terry knew this was the Ultimate Truth. And he changed his vote. Funny thing is, he didn't really mean to, but he changed a lot of votes.

The Three Judicators all changed their votes, too. "Let's face it," said Judicator Sam, "This guy knows the Truth, with a capital 'T'! I'm just really wise, and there is a difference between being wise and knowing the Truth."

Everyone agreed that was a very wise thing to say.

Dan changed his vote because he knew Terry was right, and frankly, he wasn't going to bet on getting any homework done now anyway. At least today.

Isabella, who had never understood why adults were so freaking dumb anyway, decided to change her vote, simply because it made sense to smack some sense into these people. Besides, having Aliens around could be fun.

Ava was asked if she wanted to change her vote, and this time she said "Thpppp," which everyone agreed didn't mean anything, so they just left it.

Jack changed her vote out of exasperation. She didn't have a high tolerance for this sort of thing.

And so it was agreed. Earth was to be informed of it's minuteness sooner than later. The details of which would be pounded out at a future date. The Judicators also agreed that the Tribunal After Party would be thrown at the Atomic Cat in the Milky Way. Sooner than or, though, Earth was going to get the news.

And the Party was on.

Even Premiere Josh came and had a drink.

This is really when I started to find out the details to the Story. Everyone (except the kids, they had to go to bed) was getting drunk and telling their side of the story and having a good old time, and the whole time I was thinking to myself:
"This would make a great book."

Lucky me, lucky you!

CHAPTER 36
END OF THE BEGINNING, AND VICE VERSA

The morning after the Party, everyone began leaving to go their own way, most of us back to Earth, because we didn't want to miss out on all the fun. Most of us agreed that we should get together when the Big Thing was going to happen for everyone else. Preferably somewhere safe from rioting Humans. Maybe Nebraska.

Dan donated his supply of oatmeal to the Aliens who weren't coming back for now. He also told the Judicators not to come back the second week in March, he had some tests then, and didn't want "any shit going down" at that time. They said they would see what they could do.

Neil and Tony decided it was time for another concert or movie or something, all this time off had done nothing but get them in trouble, axioms about idle hands and all. They called their agent to see what they had up next. They also told him he needed to find spots for their new friends, Joe and Anthony, who were definitely interested in doing a project with Tony and Neil, of all Beings.

Jaqueline, Isabella, and Ava all went back to Earth, but were told they just had to stop at Epsilon Centuri, which had a really killer water slide park.

Greg and Terry both decided that they would start exploring. Due to their help, they were given a ship and some funds, and told to get cracking, maybe in go to the Great Wall (not the one in China, but the one at the Edge of the Universe) and work their way back in. There was lots to see.

Premiere Josh went back to making sure the Galaxy Stayed in working order. Justin went to work on Plans for a newer, bigger, better, cooler Atomic Cat, destined to be built in New York City.

And me, I went and saw a few things Here, a few things There. Visited Delphini and stayed with the Three Bees. Nice. Lots of water. Saw a few other places other Beings told me I couldn't miss, and then headed back to Earth.

I just got back yesterday.

CHAPTER 37
THE REAL END

The stars, every night, twinkle high above. The night sky only hints at the vastness that is the Galaxy. On a really clear night, you can see the haze of starfields behind starfields, and that feeling of smallness wells up inside you, and your mind reaches out, trying to touch the edge of that great unknown. Then your mind wanders, reaching into something just as vast as the Galaxy. Imagination. And now, with your Imagination, paired with the suggestive medium that is a Story, you, gentle reader of this particular Story, can look up to those same stars, and thank them kindly that you were not vaporized by a Terrelian Snippet, or shot with a shat gat. And that you really truly understand the values of a high fiber diet.

You can finish this story in a bit, and go about your life, doing whatever it was that you did before, and believing whatever you believed before, and so on and so forth.

You may recall that in the beginning of this Story, I told you this Story can only do one thing for you. That is make you think. I hope the Story made you laugh a couple times, and I hope the Story made you pause a couple times, and I hope the Story made you mad a couple times, and I hope, in the End, you liked the Story.

I hope you identified with a Character or two, I hope you identified with a situation or two. And in the End, I hope you enjoyed yourself.

Maybe you read the Story in one sitting. Maybe you read the Story in 36 sittings, some of them on the toilet. Maybe you started reading the Story and didn't finish it till a month later. Maybe you started the Story and skipped to the End, and that's just plain shameful.

But in the End, I just hope it made you think.

The Galaxy we live in, let alone the Universe we live in, is so monstrously huge that even the Circle of Time has to give it a nod every now and then.

We live in such a small part, and on such a small scale, and frankly, for the most part, in such petty ways, that you can't help but wonder why. And if you aren't stopping to think about why, just once a day, maybe you ought to, if just for a moment.

What would the world be like, if all of a sudden, everyone realized that we really are all the same, and even if someone had four arms and two heads and three asses and believes that it was created by a tube of Chapstick, that it really wouldn't matter in the Grand Scheme of things?

If what I have said is true, if this Story is not fiction, but fact, and all of these things happened, and you were presented with the irrevocable Truth, evidence beyond reproach, like say, being abducted by Aliens, would that change you? Do you think it would change anyone? Everyone? The day after, would you wake up and say to yourself with a laugh, "Crap, no reason to sweat the small stuff anymore!" People are always sweating the small stuff first, and the big stuff later, but maybe if just didn't sweat at all, the big stuff wouldn't be so big?

The thing is, and you've heard if from me before, is there are Aliens. All over the place. And they think you're silly. It doesn't matter what for, or when for...they just do.

And the real problem is, one of these days, after you laughed and said, "Oh, Os, you fool, whatever." (Which means "I don't care" in any language.) After that, those Aliens are going to show up. They told me they would, and I don't think they had any reasons to tell stories about it. And how are Humans going to react when they find out about all this? Looting and Rioting probably. Political referendums to ban Aliens from entering the Solar System. A whole planet unified against a new threat, even though the only thing the Aliens really want are Grand Pianos, blue jeans, and maybe now, some oatmeal.

There will be talk show hosts with crazy people, and the Leaders of the world will all fight about who gets to talk to the Aliens and who doesn't. Of course, we will probably be infinitely interested in Alien Technology and Weaponry. And, of course, who can have it and who can't. We will probably end up pissing off our new possible friends because we have to act like the masses, instead of like the intelligent individuals we can be. And then the Aliens will wish they'd have just left well enough alone, and other Aliens will say that they should have just let the Terrelians vaporize us.

And you know what? I voted yes.

I voted yes, and came back here to tell you all about it, so when it happens maybe, just maybe, we can not let the entire Human Race down because we just can't get along with anybody.

And then, on the other hand, this whole Story could just be social commentary. Comedic satire.

And if that's the case, you can just disregard the parts you want to, and remember the parts you likes and that stayed in keeping with what you already believed.

And that's fine, too.

I'm not the boss of you.

The problem with Humans, as you may already know, isn't that we don't have anything good about us. It's not that we are stupid. It's not that we don't have a lick of common sense. I'm telling you what it's not, because I happen to know how often it seems like the above is absolutely, without revocation, true.

We have our problems.

The issue at hand here is potential. The rest of the Universe knows we have it. We know we have it. It's just that too often, the people in charge look to the small picture. I'd love to make up excuses, but usually, it's stupidity and greed.

But things are changing. Not because they have to, or don't have to, but simple because we have no choice in the matter. We have no choice because change is the nature of the Universe.

It's not going to happen because of Destiny, but it certainly is going to happen for a reason.

Maybe we can learn to get along. Maybe we can stop killing each other and ourselves. Maybe we can start living with the next century in mind instead of the next week.

If everyone else in the Galaxy can do it, so can we Humans.

However, I happen to know the Truth, at least in this matter. It's coming. Humanity will realized it's just a drop in the bucket. Who knows how long it's going to take. Could be 10, could be 100. That's how long it took us to finally tell people smoking was bad for them, so who knows.

We just need to realize that we are not that important as individuals. Once that happens…well…

What comes next remains to be seen.

THE END

(FOR NOW)